Born in 1945, Simon Brett was educated at Dulwich College and Wadham College, Oxford, where he gained a First Class Honours degree in English. A great many of his published works are crime novels, including the Charles Paris, Mrs Pargeter and Feathering series.

Simon was chairman of the Crime Writers Association from 1986 to 1987 and of the Society of Authors from 1995 to 1997. In 2014 he was the recipient of the CWA's prestigious Diamond Dagger award. He lives near Arundel in West Sussex and is married with three grown-up children, one grandson, one granddaughter, and four cats.

## Also by Simon Brett

*Blotto, Twinks and the Ex-King's Daughter*
*Blotto, Twinks and the Dead Dowager Duchess*
*Blotto, Twinks and the Rodents of the Riviera*
*Blotto, Twinks and the Bootlegger's Moll*

# BLOTTO,
# TWINKS
### and the
## Riddle of
## the Sphinx

# SIMON BRETT

Constable • London

CONSTABLE

First published in Great Britan by C&R Crime,
an imprint of Constable & Robinson Ltd., 2013

This paperback edition published by Constable in 2014

Copyright © Simon Brett, 2013

3 5 7 9 10 8 6 4 2

The moral right of the author has been asserted.

A CIP catalogue record for this book
is available from the British Library.

ISBN: 978-1-4721-0304-8 (paperback)
ISBN: 978-1-4721-0313-0 (ebook)

Printed and bound in Great Britain by
CPI Group (UK) Ltd., Croydon, CR0 4YY

Constable
is an imprint of
Constable & Robinson Ltd
100 Victoria Embankment
London EC4Y 0DY

An Hachette UK Company
www.hachette.co.uk

www.littlebrown.co.uk

*To Tony and Judie*

# 1

# Money Worries Again!

'I'm frightfully sorry,' said Blotto, 'but what do you mean when you say "investments"?'

Mr Crouptickle looked quizzical. Doing this gave him no problem. He was wearing the kind of pince-nez in which it was virtually impossible not to look quizzical. Their pressure on his nose seemed to have an undue effect, as if they were responsible for squeezing his desiccated frame into his thin black suit. 'I'm sorry, milord?'

'Well, I've heard of "vestments" . . . kind of dresses worn by clerical boddos. Do they wear "investments" too? Or then again I've heard of "vests". Are these "investment" flipmadoodles rather like that?' asked Blotto.

Betraying no outward emotion, the Tawcester Towers 'man of business' sighed inwardly. This was clearly going to be a long morning.

He had been summoned to the Blue Morning Room by the Dowager Duchess of Tawcester, and a summons from her might never be ignored. Behind her granite features, the old matriarch appeared to be keeping up with what he was telling them. And there was no doubt that the daughter, Lady Honoria Lyminster, was taking in every word. She really was a stunning young woman, with silver-blonde hair, azure eyes and the kind of angelic figure that made the other angels jealous. Had Mr Crouptickle been of a more elevated class, he would have fallen instantly in love with her – that's what all the young toffs did. But he knew his place. Mere 'men of business' could not aspire to fall in love with members of the aristocracy. The very idea was redolent of the foul whiff of Socialism.

So two-thirds of his audience was understanding every word he said. But when it came to the Dowager Duchess's younger son, Lord Devereux Lyminster, known universally to his peers as 'Blotto' . . . yes, it was going to be a long morning.

'Are you saying you have never heard the word "investment", milord?'

'Well, I suppose I am. Certainly doesn't tickle the old memory glands.'

'An "investment", sir, is an asset or object that is purchased in the hope that it will generate income or appreciate in the future.'

'Ah,' said Blotto. But between his thatch of blond hair and dazzling blue eyes the lines of puzzlement remained. 'Could you spell it out to me a bit more, sort of uncage the ferrets, as it were?'

'Erm . . . Well, milord . . .' Mr Crouptickle was stumped. He couldn't think how to make his definition any more clear.

'Perhaps an example might help, Blotto me old pair of sugar tongs,' said Lady Honoria Lyminster, known universally to her peers as 'Twinks', who was ever ready to help her less intellectually gifted brother out of a gluepot. 'I mean, say you were to buy a racehorse for a couple of thousand guineas . . .'

Blotto nodded eagerly. At last someone was talking his language.

'And say the nag happened to win a big race . . . the Derby, let's say . . .'

Another enthusiastic nod.

'Well, should you wish to sell it thereafter, its value would have considerably increased. Is that clear?'

The furrows had reappeared on Blotto's brow. 'Not really.'

'Why not, me old butter dish?'

'Because if I had a horse that won the Derby, there's no way I'd sell it for all the nuts in Brazil.'

'No, but say someone less loyal than you were to be the Derby-winner owner . . . and he were to sell it, what then?'

'Well, I'd say he was a bit of a stencher.'

'Maybe, but you do understand the principle that the horse that had been bought for two thousand guineas and subsequently won the Derby had appreciated?'

'What, appreciated winning the Derby?'

'No,' Twinks continued patiently. 'Appreciated in value.' She spelled it out. 'Was – worth – more – money.'

'Ah.'

'Well, that's what an investment is. You buy something with a view to making more money when you sell it.'

'Right.' Blotto nodded slowly. 'Yes, I've caught up with your drift.' A new thought came to him. 'So the boddos who've got these "investment" wodjermabits, they make a lot of money, do they?'

'Investment,' said Mr Crouptickle in a tone that was almost testy, 'is the basis of capitalism.'

'Ah.' Blotto thought for a moment. 'What's "capitalism"?'

The man of business wearily prepared himself for another explanation, but before he could utter it was interrupted by the foghorn voice of the Dowager Duchess. 'Blotto doesn't need to know things like that, Crouptickle.' (It would never have occurred to Her Grace to address him by anything other than his surname. People of that class of

3

minor professionals – accountants, solicitors, doctors and so on – did not merit the dignity of a 'Mr'. And the idea that they might possess Christian names was frankly ridiculous.) 'My son has been brought up in an entirely proper way for someone of his breeding, which means he knows that talking about money is vulgar.'

'Yes, Your Grace,' said the accountant humbly, just having had his complete raison d'être relegated to the darkest outer circle of unacceptability.

'Proceed, Crouptickle,' the Dowager Duchess continued, 'with what you were telling us. And if Blotto doesn't understand all the details . . . well, it won't be the first time.'

Son smiled gratefully at mother. Generous of her to say something so nice about him. Though, as was proper for someone of her class, she had never indulged in any displays of affection – and certainly no physical contact – with her children, the Mater was not, to Blotto's mind, a bad old kipper.

'Very well.' The man of business squeezed the pince-nez even tighter on to his thin nose. 'You will recollect, Your Grace, that some months ago you entrusted me with the disposal of some gold bullion. You did not volunteer me the information as to where it had come from, but—'

'Nor do I intend to volunteer it now,' snapped the Dowager Duchess. 'Asking members of the aristocracy where they got their assets from is the absolute depths of bad form.'

Twinks could not help but agree with her mother on that point. Her studies of history had taught her that the acquisitiveness of the British upper classes knew no limits. Most of their property had derived from a concerted campaign of pillage and exploitation of those too feeble to fight back. And when all the pillage and exploitation had helped the monarch currently in power, that was how most of them had achieved their titles.

4

Not that Twinks felt any shadow of guilt about the situation. Though of exceptional intelligence, she knew the boundaries within which sympathy could properly be exercised. The ideas of showing compassion to the lower classes, or of embracing the dangerous concept of equality, did not even enter her extraordinarily pretty head.

'Very well, Your Grace,' said Mr Crouptickle. 'So, as I say, you asked me to dispose of this bullion of *unknown provenance.*'

Blotto smiled in blissful recollection. He knew the bullion's provenance, and that knowledge gave him a warm glow of satisfaction. Each gold ingot was stamped: 'PROPERTY OF US GOVERNMENT'. It had been acquired – Blotto did not know how – by some Mafiosi in Chicago. He had brought it back from the United States in his Lagonda, after escaping the machinations of an evil cattle baron whose ambition had been to marry Blotto off to his daughter. That match was intended to sort out Tawcester Towers's financial troubles, but the bullion had done the job just as effectively. Without getting Blotto entwined in the coils of matrimony. Beezer result all round, in his view.

'Actually, Mr Crouptickle,' said Twinks, 'I'm not sure that I like your usage of the word "dispose". That implies a rather terminal fate for the bullion ... whereas all the Mater asked you to do was to invest it.'

The man of business nodded obsequiously. 'Indeed, milady. You have made a very accurate summary of the task with which Her Grace entrusted me.'

'Can we get on with this?' the Dowager Duchess demanded with some testiness. 'I have summoned you here, Crouptickle, because there's been some infernal mix-up with the bank. The bank that has had the honour of dealing with the Lyminster family affairs for many generations. The little man who bears some title like "manager"

5

has had the impertinence to say that there is no money in the Tawcester Towers account. As a result, a cheque which I sent to my dressmaker has . . . what I believe is called in common parlance . . . *bounced*. Do you have any explanation for this unhappy state of affairs, Crouptickle?'

'I do,' the man of business replied gravely.

'Well, it had better be a spoffing good one,' said Blotto, who found he was taking a personal interest in the bars of precious metal that he had inadvertently smuggled across the Atlantic. 'We're talking about Jeroboams full of money here. I mean, that bullion must have been worth its weight in gold.'

'Exactly so, milord.'

'Well, where is it now?'

'It is with the people to whom it was sold . . . or with the people to whom they have sold it on,' came the unctuous reply from Mr Crouptickle.

'But why was it sold?' demanded Twinks. 'Gold has traditionally been a secure and appreciating asset at times of financial instability.'

When his sister came out with sentences like that, Blotto could only gape admiringly. He gaped admiringly.

'Why in the name of strawberries,' she went on, 'did you take it upon yourself to sell the bullion?'

A smug smile flickered across Mr Crouptickle's narrow features. 'I did not take anything upon myself, milady. I know my place. I am a mere functionary. I act only as instructed.'

'So who instructed you to sell the bullion?'

By way of reply, the man of business's eyes focused on his employer.

'I told him to do it,' the Dowager Duchess announced. There was no apology in her tone. Indeed she did not possess a tone that could accommodate apology.

'But why, Mater?' asked Twinks despairingly.

'I met the Duchess of Dorking at a house party. She assured me that the bottom was about to fall out of the bullion market.'

'What did she base this view on?'

'I have no idea, Twinks. But that's not the kind of question you ask a chum you've been at school with. It wouldn't be nice.'

'So the Duchess of Dorking told you to sell the bullion?'

'Exactly. And put the proceeds into stocks and shares.'

Twinks turned her doom-laden face from her mother to Mr Crouptickle. 'And that's what you did?'

'Of course.'

'Did you think it was a wise course of action?'

'It is not my place to have an opinion on a matter like that, milady.'

'But you're an accountant or something, aren't you?'

'Yes, milady.'

'So you must have opinions.'

'I may have opinions, but I would not be so presumptuous as to imagine that they were of greater validity than those of your mother.'

'So what happened to the Mater's investments?' asked Twinks wearily.

There was something approximating to satisfaction in Mr Crouptickle's voice as he replied, 'The Stock Market Crash, milady.'

# 2

# The Search for a Solution

'This really has put the crud in the crumpet,' observed
Blotto. 'When I brought that bullion back from America, I
thought Tawcester Towers's financial problems were off
the gaff for good.'

'So did I,' agreed Twinks. 'Whereas now it seems we're
up an even taller gum tree with no ladder.'

They were sitting in her boudoir. She'd used her newfangled electric kettle to make cocoa for them. They had
spent many times together in that room, but rarely in such
low spirits.

'And it does actually seem,' Twinks went on, 'that the
whole clangdumble was the Mater's fault.'

Blotto was shocked. 'I say, rein in the old roans for a
moment, old girl. Criticising the Aged P is a bit beyond the
barbed wire. Not the gentlemanly thing.'

'In case you hadn't noticed,' said Twinks, 'I'm not a
gentleman. I'm a lady.'

Her brother blushed. Twinks was such a modern girl,
talking about things like that. He was vaguely aware that
there was a difference between male and female, but it
wasn't something he'd ever heard mentioned out loud.

'Anyway,' Twinks continued, 'it doesn't really matter

who was responsible – though there's no doubt it was in fact the Mater—'

'Now I'm not sure you should say things like—'

She steamrolled over him. 'What is important is how we extricate ourselves from this particular treacle tin.'

Blotto's expression changed. Worries about criticising the Mater dissipated, to be replaced by a look of benign anticipation. 'So what are we going to do?'

'Sorry?'

'To extricate ourselves from this particular treacle tin?'

'I don't know.'

'What? Oh come on, Twinks, don't play card tricks on me with this one. We've got a problem – and I know in that situation you can always be relied on to have a solution to it, zappety-ping.'

'Well, in this instance I haven't.'

Blotto looked closely at his sister, searching for the twinkle in her azure eye. Surely she wasn't serious? Surely sorting out the current glitch wasn't beyond the capacity of her grade A brainbox? 'Are you sniggling me, Twinks?' he asked.

'No, I'm not. I genuinely haven't got a mouse squeak of an idea how we're going to get out of this one.'

'Oh,' said Blotto. He couldn't deny a feeling of disappointment. From the nursery onwards, whenever he had encountered a wrinkle in the sunny fabric of his life, his sister had always been there to iron it out.

There was a long silence. Sister looked as despondent as brother. Blotto decided he must take the initiative to bring a little cheer back into their lives. 'You know, Twinks me old boot-blacking brush,' he began, 'I recently talked to a common person . . .'

She looked aghast. 'How in the name of Denzil did that happen?'

'I was travelling by train.'

9

'But surely you were in a first-class carriage?'

'Oh, indeed I was. But you'd be amazed by the kind of oikish spongeworms who can afford to travel in first-class carriages these days. You'll never guess what this fellow I met did for a living . . . ?'

'Amaze me!'

'He was a politician.'

The anticipated expression of contempt did not form on Twinks's beautiful face. 'You mean he was a member of the House of Lords? Because our brother Loofah, the Duke of Tawcester, sometimes attends the Upper—'

'No, this chap was a member of the House of Commons.'

This time the delayed disgust did flood the fair features. 'But why on earth did you speak to him, Blotto? Had you been introduced?'

'No, we hadn't. The boddo just started talking to me.'

'Great whiffling water rats! You mean he initiated conversation with someone he'd never met before?'

'That's about the volume of it.'

'What a stencher!'

'I was a bit face-flipped, I must say.'

'But what possible reason could the lump of toadspawn have had to talk to you?'

'Apparently the stencher in question is running for Parliament. I think he thought I might be one of his constituents.'

'What, he might get a vote out of you?'

'I think that was his ruse.'

'And does the constituency he's standing for actually cover Tawcester Towers?' Although Twinks was widely read in international affairs, it had never occurred to her that anything of interest might be happening in the politics right on her doorstep.

'Apparently so,' her brother replied.

She relaxed. 'Well then, he didn't have to worry, did he?'

'Sorry? Not on the same page, Twinks me old wash-board ... ?'

'Well, he's already got your vote. The Lyminster family have voted Tory ever since party politics began. We virtually invented the Tory party.'

'Maybe, but—'

'We're right, and we've always been right – in every sense,' Twinks continued forcefully. 'Common people should never be allowed near to the business of government. We all know that. The only people who have the skills to rule are those who also have the right to rule – in other words, people like us.'

'But—

'You're not disagreeing with me, are you, Blotters?'

'No, no, what you're saying is absolutely tickey-tockey. And of course now you ladies have got the vote too, haven't you?' He couldn't help giggling. 'Who'll they be giving it to next? Children? Dogs? Cats?'

His sister turned on him a look of uncharacteristic sternness. 'Blotto, you are trivialising one of the most important political developments of this or any century.'

'Well, I don't know about "trivialising".' He was speaking no more than the truth. He'd never heard the word before. Blotto found himself giggling again as he went on. 'But it does seem a bit banana-shaped, doesn't it ... I mean, the idea of women troubling their pretty heads about votes and politics and ... ?'

The intensity of the look now being beamed from his sister's azure eyes dried up his words at source. Must remember, he gave himself a memo, clearly women's suffrage was one of the few areas of life where Twinks didn't see the joke. Probably a subject to steer the dinghy away from in the future.

'Anyway,' he said, shrewdly diverting the conversation

11

in another direction, 'about this boddo on the train, you've got the wrong end of the treacle spoon.'

'Oh?'

'Talking about him already having my vote. And,' he reminded himself, 'your vote as well. You see, that wasn't the point I was making about him.'

'Then what was it?' asked Twinks, still testy.

Blotto was silent, not wanting to break the news too suddenly. Then he announced, 'This particular pineapple I met on the train wasn't a Tory.'

'Great Wilberforce! What was he then? A Liberal?'

'No.' Blotto paused again before saying the word. 'He was a Socialist.'

Now Twinks was not the kind of girl who'd ever before had the need for smelling salts. Her reckless insouciance in the face of danger had frequently been commented on. And she was a lot braver than the raft of sporting and military heroes who so regularly fell in love with her.

But these were exceptional circumstances. Never in her life had Twinks been subjected to a shock on such a scale.

Fortunately Blotto remembered that in her sequinned reticule his sister always kept a bottle of sal volatile to revive females less intrepid than herself. It was a matter of moments to have the top off and be waving the restorative beneath his sister's fine nose. Within seconds she shook her delicate head, setting up ripples in her ash-blonde hair, and was herself again.

'Are you saying, Blotto,' she asked, 'that the constituency in which we, the Lyminster family, live, might perhaps one day be represented in the Houses of Parliament by a Socialist?'

He gave a sombre nod to confirm the awful possibility. Another long silence ensued while his sister digested the information. 'It'll never happen,' she announced, but her customary assurance had momentarily deserted her.

She brought her focus back to the matter in hand. 'You still haven't told me, Blotto me old curry-comb, why you began telling me this saga of the six-faced Socialist . . .'

'Ah well, no, you see, the thing is, we were talking about money, weren't we? Or rather the lack of it so far as Tawcester Towers is concerned. And I was struck by something that this potential Member of Parliament boddo said to me.'

'What did the running sore say to you?'

'Well, when he found out who I was—'

'You let the little filch-features know who you were?'

'Yes.'

'Why?'

'Because he asked me.'

'That was no reason to answer him. Slimers like that should either recognise members of the aristocracy or keep their verminous little mouths shut!' Twinks could sound worryingly like her mother at times. And Blotto had never heard her being quite so vindictive towards the lower classes. Generally, like most people of her breeding, Twinks just basked in her obvious superiority over the rest of the world and took no notice of those less privileged. In a rare moment of perception, Blotto concluded that her current viciousness was born of frustration. His sister was unused to not finding an instant solution to a problem, – viz. the financial crisis facing Tawcester Towers – and it was not an experience she was enjoying.

'Anyway,' she went on grumpily, 'when he did find out who you were, what did he say?'

'Ah, now this was interesting. He said I was a dinosaur. "A dinosaur in the twentieth century," he said. Which I thought was rather odd, because I didn't think there were any dinosaurs in the twentieth century. I thought they all died out yonks back. What's more, I've seen pictures of dinosaurs and, so far as I can tell, I don't look anything like

13

them. I haven't got any of those funny horn things sticking out. Or scaly skin, come to that.' Blotto had never been very at ease with metaphors. 'But that's what the oik said. And then he went on, "Come the revolution, you'll be one of the first ones up against the wall!" I thought it was a bit of a rum baba that he said that too.'

'Why?'

'Well, I wouldn't have expected a stencher like that to have heard of the Eton Wall Game.'

'Erm, Blotto me old moustache-curler, I'm not sure that's what he—'

'Anyway, that wasn't the important thing the filcher said.'

'So what was?'

'He said, "You must be rolling in it." Took me a moment to work out what he thought I was rolling in, but then I decided he meant money.'

'I think he probably did.'

'And then he went on, "Families like yours make all your money from the sweat of the brows of honest working men, build yourself dirty great piles like Tawcester Towers – there's no justice. You must be rolling in it."' Blotto slurped down the last of his cocoa with considerable relish, then beamed at his sister. 'See?'

'See what?'

'Well, if an uneducated trumble like that reckons that we're rolling in it . . .'

'Ye-es.'

'Then that must mean that we really are rolling in it. Mustn't it?'

'Erm,' said Twinks. 'Actually, Blotters . . . it's not quite as simple as that.'

14

# 3

# Men of Business

The two siblings arranged to meet Mr Crouptickle again, this time without their mother present. Since they did not wish the Dowager Duchess to suspect that they were going behind her back, they met away from Tawcester Towers at the accountant's office in Tawsford, the county town of Tawcestershire.

Mr Crouptickle's premises were in a square Georgian building made in the biscuit-coloured local stone. There was an air of opulence about the whole set-up. He had a large number of secretaries working in an outer office on the latest typewriters. However much his clients might be feeling the pinch, it was clear that Mr Crouptickle himself was doing very nicely, thank you.

The coffee he had ordered came in a Georgian silver pot, and the bone-china cups would not have disgraced Tawcester Towers. A secretary poured for them, and then left the meeting room.

'So, milord, milady . . . to what do I owe this pleasure?'

His manner was not the appropriate one for a minor functionary addressing his betters. There was an air of smugness about him, almost of condescension. As though he were in some way superior to them. Blotto and Twinks bridled. From the Crusades onwards, the Lyminsters had taken a pretty dim view of people imagining they were superior to them.

'The fact is,' said Twinks, 'we would like a little clarification about the process by which a large amount of gold bullion was transmogrified into worthless stocks and shares.'

The man of business shrugged with elaborate helplessness. 'I'm afraid that is the way of the world, milady. Since recent unfortunate events in the United States, international markets have become extremely volatile.'

'So are you actually saying,' asked Blotto, 'that the jingle-jangle from the sale of the bullion has all gone?'

Another helpless shrug. 'How I wish I could say that was not the case. But I'm afraid it is.' No one had ever issued an apology that sound less apologetic.

'Surely, though, Mr Crouptickle,' insisted Twinks, 'as our mother's man of business, it is your job to give her advice on financial matters.'

'Indeed it is, milady. But have you ever known your mother to show much aptitude for taking advice?'

The question was unanswerable. Dammit, the man was right.

'And since,' he went on, 'she doesn't listen to advice, but keeps ordering me to do things, my job is reduced to the single function of following her instructions. Do you think I would be well advised to question such instructions from your mother?'

Blotto let out a heartfelt 'No.' He remembered once in the nursery questioning his mother's instructions. He could still feel the humiliation of the beating with the back of a hairbrush that the Dowager Duchess had delegated his nanny to administer.

'So,' the man of business continued, 'when your mother instructed me to sell the gold bullion and invest the proceeds in stocks and shares – whatever my own views on the inadvisability of such a course might have been – I had no alternative but to follow them.'

Twinks looked downcast. 'I was rather afraid that was what you'd say. But I thought the question was worth asking.'

'I'm sorry,' said Mr Crouptickle, not sounding sorry at all. In fact sounding almost gleeful.

'So what else can we do?' asked Blotto. 'Get one of those mortgage flipmadoodles?'

'If only you could,' came the unctuous reply. 'But Tawcester Towers is already mortgaged.'

'To the hilt?'

'Rather deeper than that. In fact, the estate is so deeply mortgaged even the tip of the hilt is not visible.'

'So it's down to selling the family silver, is it?'

'Ah, milady, if only that were possible . . .'

'What do you mean?'

'The family silver is allowed to stay in Tawcester Towers by special dispensation of the bank who owns it as security on previous loans.'

'And dare I ask about the family portraits in the Long Gallery?'

'I'm afraid exactly the same situation obtains with them, milady.'

'And there's nothing else we can sell?'

Mr Crouptickle spread his hands wide in a gesture of helplessness. 'Can you think of anything else you can sell?'

Twinks was forced to admit that she couldn't.

'Though we'll have a jolly good shuffle round the old place,' Blotto asserted defiantly, 'and I'm sure we'll find something. Won't we, Twinks me old pan scourer?'

For once his sister could not provide a reassuring affirmative. 'Do you have any other suggestions as to what we could do, Mr Crouptickle?' The never-before-heard quality in her voice was humility.

'I fear there is only one solution, milady.'

'And what is that?'

'To sell Tawcester Towers.'

'Sell Tawcester Towers!' said Blotto and Twinks together, too shocked to be capable of more than an echo.

'There is a market for such properties,' insinuated Mr Crouptickle. 'A few have been turned into hotels, and I'm sure that is a trend which will increase as more and more long-established families begin to feel the economic pinch.'

'An hotel?' Twinks could scarcely bring herself to say the word. 'An hotel? Are you suggesting that Tawcester Towers should be turned into an hotel?'

'And have lots of oikish spongeworms sleeping in our beds?' said Blotto.

'It is a possibility, milord.'

'No, it isn't, Crouptickle.'

'Anyway, if we were to sell Tawcester Towers,' demanded Twinks, 'where would we live?'

'I might suggest that you could move into cheap rented accommodation and get jobs.'

'No Lyminster would ever do that!' cried the unison voices of Blotto and Twinks.


Eventually a kind of compromise was agreed. Though not optimistic of the chances of finding anything worth selling, Mr Crouptickle suggested that an inventory should be made of the contents of Tawcester Towers. He pressed the button of an electric buzzer on his desk and, like an unpleasant smell borne on the wind from a distant privy, there appeared in his office another black-suited man, unbelievably even thinner than his employer. The two of them looked like a pair of praying mantises.

'May I introduce Mr Snidely? Also an accountant like myself,' said Mr Crouptickle. 'Lord Devereux Lyminster and Lady Honoria Lyminster.'

The newcomer bowed to his superiors, as obsequious as a pat of butter melting on a hot muffin. 'I am extremely honoured to be in your presence, milord, milady.'

'You certainly are,' said Twinks, a glacial version of her mother. Though not snobbish to all common people, she had a particular – and entirely appropriate – animus against those who came under the category of accountants or solicitors.

Mr Snidely turned to Mr Crouptickle. 'And what task is it which is to be entrusted to my competence?' he asked.

The man of business gave him a brief résumé of his duties. It was agreed that Mr Snidely should report to Tawcester Towers the following morning to begin the compilation of his inventory. 'And should I present myself to you, milord? Or you, milady?'

'Neither,' said Twinks, still sounding uncannily like her mother. 'You should present yourself to Grimshaw the butler.'

She didn't want people like Mr Snidely getting ideas above their station.


As they left the accountant's office and got into the Lagonda, Blotto and Twinks saw a large banner hanging outside Tawsford Town Hall which read: VOTE FOR ALFRED SPROCKETT. RALLY THIS AFTERNOON. EVERYONE WELCOME.

'And who's Alfred Sprockett when he's got his spats on?' asked a disconsolate Twinks.

'Toad-in-the-hole!' said Blotto as a recollection came to him. 'I've met the stencher!'

'You've met him? I can't believe it, Blotters. You went to Eton, and you're telling me you've actually met someone called Alfred Sprockett?'

'He was the four-faced filcher I encountered on the train.'

'The Socialist?'

'Yes.'

Twinks looked again at the Town Hall, and observed that a lot of depressed-looking men in flat caps and women in battered hats were filing in through the entrance. Suddenly she was more cheerful. 'Larksissimo!' she cried. 'His rally's starting right now. Let's go in and find out what we're up against.'

'Toad-in-the-hole,' said Blotto, as ever amazed by his sister's daring.

# Dangerous Talk

Blotto had never been inside the Town Hall, though his sister had attended a few occasions when their mother was required to patronise the local populace. Flower shows, charity teas, mayoral inaugurations, wakes after the funerals of Tawsford dignitaries ... all such events were thought to be given an added lustre by the presence of the Dowager Duchess of Tawcester. The lady herself rationed such appearances as much as was possible, and when prevailed on to attend, fixed her craggy face in an expression of undisguised disgust, as though she were offended by the aromas arising from the local citizenry. As indeed she was. But local reports, either in gossip or the newspapers, always commented on how 'gracious' Her Grace had been.

To the surprise of Blotto and Twinks, it was clear that Alfred Sprockett was a popular man in the community. There was hardly a spare seat to be had inside the Town Hall. And on entrance their nostrils were immediately assailed by the kind of odours that so offended their mother. Twinks, whose olfactory sensibility was as well developed as all her other senses, was able to identify a good many of the trades pursued by members of the throng. Tanners were certainly present, also men involved in the sewerage industry. She identified the smoky tang of blacksmiths, foundrymen and charcoal burners.

Nor were the females present odour-free. Cooks brought with them the fatty stench of the kitchen, housemaids the whiff of furniture polish, nurses the miasma of disinfectant. Though the part of Twinks so supportive of women's suffrage approved of their attending a political rally, her delicate nose was less enthusiastic.

Predominating over all the other aromas, however, from men or women, were the emanations of the farmyard. It was abundantly evident that many of those present had only recently left the company of cattle, horses and particularly pigs. The soil of which they were sons and daughters clung to their boots and garments.

Twinks found it all absolutely fascinating.

She and her brother were unaware of the rather old-fashioned looks that were being cast in their direction. They had been brought up to be unaware of anyone who wasn't of comparable breeding to their own. Members of Alfred Sprockett's audience were as invisible to them as the majority of the Tawcester Towers servants (with the honourable exception of Corky Froggett the chauffeur).

So it would never have occurred to either of them that they might look out of place at the gathering in Tawsford Town Hall. True, no one else present was wearing full shooting tweeds and a brown homburg like Blotto. Nor were any of the other women sporting above-the-knee grey silk dresses, silver mink coats and cloche hats like Twinks. But neither of the siblings noticed these differences. They were, in some senses, great egalitarians.

Instead they focused their attention on the eloquence of the occasion's principal attraction, Alfred Sprockett. In his account to his sister of their encounter in a first-class railway carriage, Blotto had not provided any physical description of the gentleman (if that was the right word in

22

the circumstances?), so she had not been prepared for what she saw on the stage of Tawsford Town Hall.

The speaker, blessed with a very round body and a very round head, bore an uncanny resemblance to a cottage loaf to which small arms and legs had been appended. A pelmet of ginger hair ran around the back of his cranium, and on his upper lip a moustache of the same shade erupted like weeds from an untended pavement. Watery blue eyes bulged under ginger brows and his face was of a combustible redness yet to be attained by any boiled lobster. To compound his unattractiveness to Blotto and Twinks, Alfred Sprockett's accent derived from the North of England, immediately excluding him from the list of people whom it might be appropriate for them to meet.

The redness of his countenance might well have been explained by the vehemence of his oratory. People have frequently been described as tub-thumpers, but the manner of Alfred Sprockett's rhetoric threatened to smash to smithereens any tub incautious enough to get in his way.

'Brothers and sisters . . .' he was saying as Blotto and Twinks squeezed their way into the odiferous crowd at the back of the hall.

'Toad-in-the-hole!' whispered Blotto to his sister as he looked around the throng. 'He's got a big family if they're all his brothers and sisters. I suppose that class do breed like rabbits, don't they?'

'No, Blotters, I don't think—'

'Brothers and sisters . . .' Alfred Sprockett repeated, 'for too long the workers of this country have been downtrodden by the iron heel of the privileged classes. For too long the sweat of our brows has paid for their extravagances.'

'I didn't know sweat was legal tender,' murmured a bemused Blotto.

'Ssh,' said Twinks.

'For too long the common man has had no say in the government of this great country of ours. For too long we have been excluded from the decisions of state. Well . . .' Alfred Sprockett's face turned ever pucer as he approached a minor climax '. . . it is time for that to change!'

The level of vociferous enthusiasm with which this sentence was greeted surprised both Blotto and Twinks. The previous encounters they had shared with common people had been considerably quieter. Those who had visited Tawcester Towers knew the appropriate demeanour in the presence of their betters. 'Only speak when spoken to' was the invariable rule. It was rather bizarre – and maybe a little unsettling – to hear such volume of sound from the common populace.

'So let's just go into a little detail,' bellowed Alfred Sprockett, 'about what we want to change. Shall we do that?' The crowd roared their approval of the suggestion. 'So let me ask you a few questions . . .'

Blotto felt uneasy. Those words 'So let me ask you a few questions . . .' had ominous associations for him. They took him straight back to the schoolrooms of Eton where the beady eyes of the beaks regularly singled him out to see how much attention he had been paying to their lessons. And the answer to that was invariably: very little. Blotto's mind was just not very good at assimilating facts. He had always had great difficulty dragging it away from dreams of the cricket pitch and the hunting field. Nor could he ever quite be convinced of the essential importance of mental arithmetic, Latin declensions and French irregular verbs.

So some atavistic fear within him made him very nervous about the questions Alfred Sprockett threatened to ask. There was a silence before the first one was posed. Then it came. 'Do we want to continue with a tiny percentage of this country's population owning a huge percentage of its land?'

24

Relief flooded through Blotto. Toad-in-the-hole, he cheered himself, if all of the questions are going to be this easy . . . 'Yes!' he cried in reply.

'Do we want,' Alfred Sprockett asked, 'people who have inherited their money to have more power than those who have earned it by the sweat of their brows?'

Again Blotto had no difficulty in replying with a resounding 'Yes!' (though he did wonder why the man kept going on about sweat so much).

'Do we want,' came the next cry from Alfred Sprockett, 'the poor and the infirm to be ignored while the rich enjoy their lives of banquets, hunting, shooting and fishing?'

The answer to this was obviously another 'Yes', though Blotto did wish he had the opportunity to point out that the residents of Tawcester Towers did in fact do a lot for the poor and infirm on their estate. Stale bread and soup made from the bones and internal organs of game birds were distributed to their humble cottages with some frequency, and they were all invited to join the Lyminster family for a single glass of sherry on Christmas Eve. But the noisy rally in Tawsford Town Hall didn't seem to be a suitable forum in which he could make these points. The charitable work of the owners of Tawcester Towers would have to go unacknowledged.

The manner in which Alfred Sprockett posed his questions had been building in intensity. His face was now so empurpled that he looked close to spontaneous combustion. 'Do we want,' he demanded with a dramatic flourish, 'to return to the feudal system?'

Blotto's 'Yes!' in response to this was so loud that for the first time the aspiring politician became aware of his presence.

He pointed a stubby red finger towards the aristocratic pair. 'So look who we have here,' he cried. 'Spies in our midst! You have a nerve to come in here.'

'We have as much right,' shouted Twinks indignantly, 'to be here as anyone else in the hall. Doesn't the banner outside say: "EVERYONE WELCOME"? So does "EVERYONE" not include us?'

'No!' bellowed Alfred Sprockett. '"EVERYONE" means everyone who does an honest day's work for their living – except of course for those unfortunate brothers and sisters who are unable to find jobs due to the greed and exploitative practices of people like you.'

'Are you saying,' asked a glacial Twinks, 'that my brother and I are not welcome here?'

'I am saying,' roared Alfred Sprockett in response, 'that your type aren't welcome anywhere! And what's more, your type won't be around much longer! This country's changing, and soon the filthy rich like you will no longer be living in places like Tawcester Towers, battening off the sweat of the working classes.' (Sweat again, thought Blotto.)

'There's a revolution already under way in this country and when it finally comes to fruition, you two will be first up against the wall.'

'He's a bit of a voidbrain,' said Blotto, as they walked away from the baying multitude in Tawsford Town Hall.

'Sorry?' Twinks was preoccupied.

'That Alfred Sprockett – he said it again, didn't he? About the wall. And he included you, being up against the wall. What a clip-clop! He ought to know that girls don't play the Eton Wall Game.'

But his sister didn't seem to be listening. 'You know, Blotto me old fish-gutter,' she said gloomily, 'this whole country is going to hell in a hansom cab.'

# 5

# Adventures in the Attic

Blotto's and Twinks's childhood had lacked some of the things voguish psychologists deem to be necessary for the developing young – like parental affection. The Dowager Duchess was much more interested in her dogs and horses than she ever was in her progeny, and it was a moot point whether her husband, the late Duke, was even aware that he had further children after the continuity of the title had been secured by the birth of Loofah. The only human contact the siblings had experienced had been with nurses, nannies and maids.

Nor had their nursery been free of corporal punishment – their nanny had more than one way of using a hairbrush and possessed a mean skill with her ear twisting, arm pinching and knuckle rapping. Hazards of their young lives had also included regular sendings to bed without supper and frequent washings out of their mouths with soap and water.

But the one advantage Blotto and Twinks had had over most other children in the entire world was the Tawcester Towers estate as their personal playground. The extensive woods and parklands had opened up infinite possibilities for adventures on their ponies – and allowed Blotto to develop his skills in cricket, running and other athletic pursuits.

But even more exciting for two spirited youngsters had been the possibilities offered by the ancestral pile of Tawcester Towers itself. At some point someone may have counted how many rooms the house contained but that total had long since been lost in the mists of history. The two youngsters could spend whole days gambolling from vaulted chamber to vaulted chamber without ever seeing another human being.

As a result they had devised many private games – or, to be strictly accurate, Twinks had devised many private games and Blotto had been happy to play his part in them. Most of the scenarios involved daring rescues from situations of unspeakable jeopardy. Generally Twinks took on the damsel-in-distress role (though there had never in the annals of history been a damsel more capable of looking after herself) and then described to her brother the devious plan by which he would have to save her life, honour or both. Blotto could rarely work out the logic of what he was meant to be doing, but he was good at blindly following instructions, particularly if those instructions involved biffing people. Since most of the games Twinks invented required his overcoming dauntingly unfair odds and pole-axing plenty of imaginary stenchers, he was as happy as a cat in a fishmonger's.

It was through these games that Blotto and Twinks developed their skills in weapon-play, climbing and escapology. Vaulted ceilings and giant staircases offered wonderful opportunities for swinging from ropes and the aristocratic siblings developed routines that would have made the average circus trapeze artist look to his laurels. The Tawcester Towers roofs, a higgledy-piggledy assemblage of turrets, spires and crenellations, also provided a wonderful training ground for feats of derring-do. Indeed, by the time the pair reached their teens, they were better versed in fieldcraft than the elite troops of His Majesty's army.

Some of their manoeuvres would be given private names – by Twinks, of course, Blotto wasn't so good on the verbal stuff. And some had proved really useful in the hair-raising adventures of their adult lives. For example, a move called a 'Double Drumski', much rehearsed on the battle-ments of Tawcester Towers, had recently saved Blotto and Twinks from being liquidised in a meat grinder in a Chicago meat-packing plant. Nor was that the only occasion when exercising some well-remembered routine had extracted them from the depths of a particularly viscous gluepot.

This familiarity with every cornice and gargoyle of their ancestral home did prompt an idea in Twinks. It wasn't a real buzzbanger of an idea, just a squiblet really, but better than nothing. And in her current state of diminished imagination, she was happy to grab at any straw which wafted her way.

She had rationalised the basic problem with the Tawcester Towers's financial situation, and indeed reduced it to one very basic conclusion. They didn't have any money.

And Twinks knew that there were only a few ways to get money. You could inherit it – which was always the best way, but the trouble with that was you could only inherit it once. You could earn it – but obviously getting jobs was out of the question for people of the Lyminsters' breeding. You could steal it – but, though that was how the first rob-ber barons had founded the family fortunes, attitudes to crime had changed over the years and stealing was no longer quite the thing.

And if none of the above methods of getting money was available, then you could possibly sell something.

29

Twinks knew that the obvious Lyminster treasures, the family silver and the portraits in the Long Gallery were, as Mr Crouptickle had so gleefully told them, all in hock. She knew too that Mr Snidely was making lists of the contents of Tawcester Towers, but she didn't have much confidence in the possibility of his unearthing anything of value. Anyway, he was starting his note-taking in the main downstairs rooms of the house. Twinks was convinced that, if there were any other objects of value hidden away, then the place to look for them would be the attics.

These dusty repositories contained the junk of many centuries. Generations of Lyminsters had accumulated incredible amounts of stuff. Some of it had had artistic merit, some of it had been entirely worthless. But most had in time met the same fate, being replaced by more new stuff and being unceremoniously manhandled by sweating servants up to the attics. These were irregularly shaped rooms, even higher up than the poky hutches in which the house's domestic staff slept. Nobody visited their musty interiors. Even Blotto and Twinks hadn't been up there since they were children, when they had played unending games of hide-and-seek.

But desperate times called for desperate measures, and nothing could have been more desperate than the current financial outlook for Tawcester Towers and its residents. So the Monday morning after their visit to Mr Crouptickle, the aristocratic siblings dug out their oldest clothes (still managing to look impossibly glamorous in them) and set out to search for treasure in the attics. They did not tell the Dowager Duchess of their plans. In fact the only person they mentioned what they were doing to was Corky Froggett, one of the Tawcester Towers chauffeurs. An ex-military man, not carrying an extra ounce of weight though well into his fifties, Froggett might be needed if there were any heavy lifting involved.

The Tawcester Towers attics could have proved a fascinating research field for a social historian. The arrival and passing of many technologies and fads were chronicled by their contents. Rusty weapons from wars lost years before were piled up, now offering more danger from tetanus than from the sharpness of their blades. Dented armour, ripped chain mail and battered shields scattered over the floor, the bodies who had felt the dents, rips and battering long dead and gone to dust. Superannuated bits and other items of horse tack hung from hooks.

And so each century was defined by its detritus. Even the most recent leavings had been in the attics long enough to be under layers of dust. From the Victorian era broken 'boneshaker' bicycles were piled up on the hoops of crinolines. Corsets tangled with birdcages. Oil lamps, upstaged and relegated by electricity, lay about in shattered profusion.

The attics also bore witness to the interests of the various dukes who had in their time presided over Tawcester Towers. All of them were called 'Rupert', though most had a nickname as well. Evidence of the fifth duke, Black Rupert's, libidinous doings lay in the attic in the form of dresses he had ripped off peasant girls. His son Rupert the Fiend's predilections were represented by a collection of opium pipes, laudanum bottles and other impedimenta for drug use. In another attic there were piles of cracking leather ledgers in which Rupert the Dull had justified the accounts and brought Tawcester Towers back from the brink of insolvency.

And it wasn't just Rupert the Libertine who had built up the massive collection of manacles and whips which filled so many rooms. Those had accumulated over many generations. There was a strong family tradition amongst the Lyminsters – as in most English aristocratic families – of shackling and flogging serfs. And that tradition had not been allowed to go into desuetude with the ending of the feudal system.

Blotto and Twinks found sifting through their family history in the attics a dispiriting business. Not because the activity reminded them of human mortality. Twinks was far too positive a person to allow such morbid thoughts into her head, and inside her brother's head there was rarely room for more than one thought at a time. And that thought was never about mortality. What was dispiriting about their search, though, was the fact that it didn't reveal anything of value.

Twinks had hoped that they might get lucky in the room containing the artefacts brought back from his Grand Tour by Rupert the Tasteless. But sadly he'd lived up to his name. While other young men of the time had filled their family homes with priceless Greek and Roman sculptures or Old Masters, Rupert the Tasteless had bought the most terrible tourist tat – bas-reliefs of winking shepherdesses, statues of dogs urinating against lamp posts and paintings of winsome kittens on gondolas. His father, Rupert the Exasperated, had had all this rubbish put straight into the attics on his son's return home. And there it had remained ever since, not even appreciating in curiosity value.

Blotto and Twinks had had a long day with very few breaks. Lunch had just been sandwiches brought up by a housemaid. Now the light outside was fading and they were conducting their search with the aid of those modern electric torches. Only one of the attic rooms remained unbreached and breaching it was proving a difficult task. Though the picklocks Twinks always kept in her sequinned reticule acted as easily as a key, the solid oak door refused to shift when unlocked, even with the full weight of Blotto's magnificent shoulders applied to it. There seemed

32

to be some obstruction on the inside. Corky Froggett was sent for with orders to bring a toolbox and crowbars.

Eventually by the combined efforts of the two men they did manage to gain entrance, though they had to take the hinges off the door to do so. The interior space was dark, but they all got a sense of large objects looming within.

Twinks directed her torch inside and, flickering across the room, its beam illuminated giant eyes, bright patterns and the occasional glint of gold leaf.

'Great whiffling water rats!' she said in an awestruck whisper. 'I think these are the treasures brought back by Rupert the Egyptologist!'

# 6

# The Treasure Revealed!

The three of them crowded into the cramped space, each one's torch beam probing the darkness, revealing the trophies brought back from Egypt in the early nineteenth century by Blotto's and Twinks's ancestor. There were statues, reliefs and ornately carved slabs. But the most striking object, in pride of place against the wall opposite the door, was an elaborately painted stone sarcophagus.

'Blimey O'Reilly!' said Corky Froggett, in his surprise forgetting to say 'milord' or 'milady'. 'What on earth does that look like?'

'A spoffing great big jelly baby,' said Blotto.

He was right. It did look like a giant jelly baby. The outline was humanoid, but the proportions were wrong for a real person. The head was too large and the feet projected out disproportionately.

But it was a beautiful artefact. The head was leonine in shape and the carved arms, bearing symbolic wands, were crossed against the chest. The whole structure was painted and its colours seemed to glow brighter than any of the surrounding archaeological finds. As soon as she had seen the sarcophagus, Twinks had gone down on her knees and started peering at two bands of markings along the exposed side.

'What are you looking at, Twinks me old banana sandwich?' asked her brother, bringing his torch beam to focus with hers.

'Look . . .' Twinks's finger traced along the top line. 'These are hieroglyphs.'

'Are they, by Denzil?' Blotto's fingers traced along the bottom line. 'So these must be loweroglyphs?'

'No,' said Twinks kindly. 'It doesn't quite work like that.'

'Oh. So what are these hiero . . . wodjermabits when they've got their spats on?'

'A hieroglyph – sometimes mistakenly called a hieroglyphic, which is of course to use the adjectival form of the word – is a component of a written language used by the ancient Egyptians. Hieroglyphs have both phonetic and logographic components.'

'Toad-in-the-hole!' said Blotto. 'Did you hear that, Corky? Phonetic and logographic, eh?'

'I did hear it certainly, milord, though I cannot claim to have understood it.'

'Oh really?' said Blotto, rather loftily. 'Can you read these hiero . . . flipmadoodles, Twinks me old carpet-beater?'

'Yes, I made a study of them last summer when I got bored with translating *David Copperfield* into Japanese.'

'Oh. Ah. Good ticket.' Blotto watched as his sister's torch beam travelled along the rows of symbols. 'And do those fozzly squiggles tell you what's inside the box?'

'I think they're more likely to tell me *who's* inside the box.'

'Well, I'll be jugged like a hare! You mean there's someone in there? Is the stencher likely to jump out and attack us?'

'That's unlikely, Blotters. He's probably been in there over two thousand years.'

'Well, I'll be snickered,' said Blotto. 'More importantly,

though, me old pineapple peeler, is this great jelly baby of any value?'

'I would say it's extremely valuable.'

'What, the whole space crammed to the collar studs with gold bullion?'

'I think that's unlikely. Its value will be more as a unique archaeological discovery.'

'Oh. Well, maybe I should open it,' suggested Blotto, 'to reveal the goodies inside?'

'I don't think that's the best idea since the mousetrap,' Twinks cautioned. 'Listen . . .' She ran her finger along the hieroglyphs as she read, '"Herein lies the great God King Pharaoh Sinus Nefertop, guarded by the spirits of the living dead. Should anyone unauthorised . . .' Twinks's voice grew softer as she struggled with the translation '. . . open the sarcophagus . . .'

'What did she say, milord?' asked Corky Froggett.

'"Open the sarcophagus".'

'Very well, milord.'

And the chauffeur, leaning forward and focusing his huge strength, got his hands under the stone lid and managed to lift it a couple of inches.

The attic room was filled with a sound like the shriek of a fox being eviscerated in the night time, just as Twinks finished the sentence she was deciphering. '. . . "he will be visited by the Curse of Pharaoh Sinus Nefertop!"'

'Oh,' said Corky Froggett, looking a little sheepish.

# 7

# A Second Opinion

The rediscovery of Rupert the Egyptologist's finds was greeted with great celebration in Tawcester Towers. An expert in the period was summoned from the Tawcestershire County Museum in Tawsford to make a preliminary inspection of the haul. (An even more expert expert would later be called from the British Museum.) The man from Tawsford, very impressed by the contents of the attic, was in no doubt that the objects would be of considerable value on the international art market.

'But,' he said as he reported his conclusions to the Dowager Duchess in the Blue Morning Room, 'works of this quality should of course not be allowed to leave the country.' (Fortunately the rather whimsical notion that such artefacts should be returned to their place of origin had not yet caught on.)

'Rather,' he continued, 'than being put up for auction and then kept under the selfishly beady eye of one American millionaire collector, they should be available to be seen by everyone in the appropriate setting of . . . say . . . Tawcester County Museum. I am sure that someone like you, Your Grace, as one of the Great and Good of the county, who has grown up respecting the values of tradition and antiquity, will have no hesitation in handing over these precious artefacts to the museum as a gift . . . ?'

'Gift?' snorted the Dowager Duchess. 'Don't talk such bloody balderdash! We will sell the lot at the first opportunity for as much money as we can possibly get for them!'


The expert who arrived from the British Museum was a small peevish Scotsman called Mr McGloam. His features were scrunched up in a permanent expression of scepticism. Blotto and Twinks recognised this because they'd by now seen the same look so often on the face of Mr Snidely, who was still making his painfully slow – and so far unrewarding – inventory of the contents of Tawcester Towers.

They had offered to stay with Mr McGloam while he made his survey of Rupert the Egyptologist's attic, but the suggestion was dismissed with something approaching brusqueness. The British Museum expert seemed to have as little respect for his betters as Alfred Sprockett; another symptom, in the view of an uncharacteristically morose Twinks, of everything that was currently wrong with the country.

Mr McGloam did, however, assure them that he would report back to the siblings when his investigations were complete. They did not at this stage want the Dowager Duchess involved in the sordid business of valuation – time enough to tell her the good news when it was confirmed – so they didn't suggest McGloam should tell them of his findings in the Blue Morning Room. Instead, Twinks proposed they should meet in the Yellow Late Afternoon Room.

And the summons came to them surprisingly quickly. Grimshaw, the Tawcester Towers butler, found Blotto in the stables where he was silently but deeply communing with his magnificent hunter Mephistopheles. Twinks was discovered in the Library, reading Kierkegaard in the original Danish. Grimshaw, accompanied by Blotto, told her that Mr McGloam was waiting for them in the Yellow Late Afternoon Room.

The wizened Scotsman looked positively gleeful as they arrived. He rubbed his thin hands together as he asked, 'So the duke who collected that lot was called Rupert the Egyptologist, was he?'

'Good ticket,' Blotto confirmed. 'Most of the Dukes of Tawcester have sort of nicknames like that.'

'Well, in his case it wasn't very apt.'

'Why?' demanded Twinks.

'In fact a better name for him might have been Rupert the Gullible.'

'What are you saying?'

'I am saying, milady, that while the duke was in Egypt he was taken for a ride.'

'Would that be on a camel?' asked Blotto. 'Or a dromedary?' he added, pleased to have got the word right.

'No, milord,' replied Mr McGloam in a manner that was more unctuous than deferential. 'I was using the expression "taken for a ride" as a metaphor.'

'Tickey-tockey,' said Blotto, as ever confused by the metaphorical.

'I could have said "cheated", "diddled", "deceived", "swindled", "bilked" or "given a bum steer".'

'Are you telling us,' asked Twinks, as ever quicker off the mark than her brother, 'that the Egyptian artefacts in the attic are not genuine?'

'That is exactly what I'm telling you, milady.'

'But the expert from the Tawcester County Museum said they were extremely valuable.'

Mr McGloam sniggered that snigger reserved by academics only for rival academics. 'I think the word "expert" might be rather overstating things in that context. I cannot imagine that a place like the Tawcester County Museum would attract the highest calibre of applicants for its staff. Anyone who was fooled by those fakes must be one step up from a congenital idiot.'

'Are you positive about that?'

'Absolutely, milady. Those dealers out in Egypt certainly saw your ancestor coming. What he bought were not even very good fakes. Mostly made of cheap timber covered with plaster. Their antiquity could be measured in days rather than millennia.'

'But why was the duke such a voidbrain?' asked Blotto.

'Heredity?' Mr McGloam suggested.

Fortunately Blotto was not bright enough to realise the rudeness of this, but the same didn't apply to his sister. Sounding dauntingly like the Dowager Duchess, she said, 'I will ask you to keep a civil tongue in your tooth-box!'

'Apologies, milady. I didn't mean—'

'Yes, you did!'

Mr McGloam looked suitably chastened. Twinks in her full fury was a pretty daunting sight. Under her critical scrutiny amorous swains who went a little too far had been known to shrivel up like ants when small boys focused sunbeams on them with a magnifying glass.

'So you are telling us, Mr McGloam,' she continued imperiously, 'that all of the duke's collection is completely worthless?'

'Ah no, I didn't say that, milady. There is one item in the attic that is of value. Of considerable value.'

'Hoopee-doopee!' said Blotto, much cheered.

'What is it?' asked Twinks.

'The sarcophagus,' replied Mr McGloam. 'So far as I can tell, from a cursory examination, that is the actual funerary container of the remains of Pharaoh Sinus Nefertop. I will obviously have to take the sarcophagus back to the British

40

Museum to run more detailed tests, but I am optimistic that it will prove to be genuine.'

'And if it is,' asked Twinks a little breathlessly, 'what might it be worth?'

Mr McGloam spread wide his thin hands in a gesture of awestruck ignorance. 'An object of such rarity is literally priceless.'

'Grandissimo!' said Twinks.

'Beezer!' said Blotto.

'And what kind of tests would you have to run on the sarcophagus?' asked Twinks.

'Well, obviously I would need to check the contents, which might be very exciting. The mummified body could be in extremely good condition if the sarcophagus has not been opened for two or three thousand years.'

'Well, actually Corky Froggett did lift the— '

With a pained expression Blotto looked down at his sister's shoe digging into his shin. But the assault did have the desired effect of shutting him up.

'What is important, of course,' said Mr McGloam, 'is that an object of this quality should not be allowed to leave the country.

'Rather,' he continued, 'than being auctioned and kept under the selfishly beady eye of one American millionaire collector, it should be available to be seen by everyone in the appropriate setting of . . . say . . . the British Museum. I am sure that someone like you, milady, as one of the Great and Good of the country, who has grown up respecting the values of tradition and antiquity, will have no hesitation in handing over this precious artefact to the museum as a gift . . . ?'

'Gift?' snorted Twinks. 'Don't talk such toffee! We will sell the thing at the first opportunity for as much money as we can possibly get for it!'

At times she could be unnervingly like her mother.

41

# 8

# A Surprise for the Lagonda

When it came to women, Blotto's nature displayed a certain reticence. Though an entirely red-blooded male, he trod warily where the fair sex was concerned. He could appreciate beauty and acknowledged that many of the women he met were real breathsappers, but his instinct was to avoid romantic entanglements – much to the disappointment of the many debutantes who so regularly fell in love with his astonishing good looks, sporting prowess and daredevil heroism (girls of that class were entirely unworried by his minimal intellectual endowments – like called to like).

But Blotto kept his distance. He knew that, as sure as a minor sniffle could lead to full-blown flu, so the smallest expression of interest in a woman could lead to matrimony. And that was a fate he was determined to avoid for as long as he possibly could. One day, he felt gloomily certain, the Dowager Duchess would decree that he'd have to get married, but he was determined to delay that day by any means at his disposal.

But though wary of the opposite sex, Blotto was not a man without strong passions. There were three things for which he had feelings passing by far the love of women (and only one of them was actually alive). The three were: his cricket bat, his hunter Mephistopheles and his Lagonda. In the presence of each of them he felt a deep sense of peace.

The Lagonda had been his companion on many of the adventures he had shared with his sister. It had taken them across Europe to Zling, the capital of Mitteleuropia. In the Lagonda they had driven to Paris and the French Riviera to rescue two paintings stolen from the Tawcester Towers Long Gallery. The car had even crossed the Atlantic when Blotto had been threatened with marriage to the daughter of Luther P. Chapstick III.

It was during its American trip that the Lagonda had undergone certain modifications at the hands of some Chicago Mafiosi. For reasons of their own convenience a secret compartment had been built into the car's chassis. The space created was large enough to accommodate two men of ample proportions (or two dead bodies of the same size). It had also proved sufficiently large to hold the precious hoard of gold bullion which Blotto and Twinks had brought back in triumph from America and which Mr Crouptickle had so unfortunately sold to buy worthless shares.

The Lagonda's return from Chicago to Tawcester Towers had been followed by much earnest discussion between Blotto and Corky Froggett as to whether they should remove the Mafia's additional feature from the car. The purists in both master and chauffeur considered that a vehicle as distinguished as a Lagonda should be kept as close as possible to the condition in which it had left the factory. But at the same time both men recognised the convenience of the hidden space. Who could say when, in the course of one of their adventures, they might need to conceal something?

At the time of the discovery of Rupert the Egyptologist's haul in the Tawcester Towers attic no decision had yet been taken and the Lagonda retained its secret compartment.

Both Corky Froggett and his master had certain rituals in their lives. A day was not complete for Blotto at his beloved Tawcester Towers if he had not spent time at some point with Mephistopheles in his stable, and if he had not given his cricket bat a loving stroke before he retired to bed.

The third of his rituals brought master and chauffeur together. Corky Froggett was a man of iron discipline and fixed habits. The army training that had turned him into a deadly killing machine had also encouraged in him a mania for cleanliness. Just as his uniform had always been immaculate, so was everything else in his life. His quarters at Tawcester Towers (which of course Blotto had never seen – it didn't do for family members to go into the servants' part of the house) was so antiseptically hygienic that even motes of dust did not dare to land on any surface there.

And this attitude – some might say compulsion – was also evident in Corky Froggett's care of the Lagonda. Though its owner was obviously 'the young master' Blotto, the chauffeur's love of the vehicle went far beyond that which the most sentimental of shepherds felt for his precious ewe-lamb. His care obviously included meticulous tuning of the wonderful engine that lay beneath the monster's sleek bonnet, but also ensured that the Lagonda's bodywork always gleamed like a jewel of polished lapis lazuli.

To achieve this effect, every morning at ten o'clock sharp Corky Froggett would begin the laborious process of cleaning the car. This was regardless of whether the car actually needed cleaning. Some chauffeurs might have just checked the bodywork to see that no impertinent speck of dust had

had the temerity to land on their charges overnight, and wipe off the offending blemish, but that was not Corky Froggett's way. For him doing anything less than the complete cleaning and valeting of the Lagonda would have been a dereliction of duty, on his scale of values a court-martial offence.

So, every morning before he began his task, like a high priest of some ancient cult preparing for a human sacrifice, Corky Froggett would lay out on the floor of the large garage which housed the precious vehicle the sacred accessories of his ritual. There were buckets of water, with which the Lagonda (with its soft-top up and windows closed) would be initially immersed, and into which cleaning cloths would subsequently be squeezed. Of the cloths themselves there was a wide range, from kitchen rags to the highest-quality chamois leathers. There was a variety of brushes of different widths to fit into the narrowest crannies between bodywork and chrome. Dubbin was there to keep the suppleness of the leather straps that held down the Lagonda's bonnet. Tins of special glass-cleaning fluids for windows and headlights stood alongside upright bottles of chrome polisher. For the thinnest of apertures which might conceal a fleck of errant soil Corky had ready the pull-through of soft rope with which he used to clean out his rifle barrel between the shooting of individual Huns during the most recent international dust-up.

It was a ritual that Blotto loved to witness, and he often organised his day so that he would be passing the garages at ten o'clock in the morning. He would then, having lit a cigarette, watch Corky Froggett go through his unchanging routine, the two men united in an act of love for the car too intense to be expressed in words.

And when the chauffeur had buffed the last piece of chrome and completed his unflinching final scrutiny of the Lagonda, he would once again salute the young master.

And Blotto, with a murmur of 'Nice work, Corky,' would move on to his next morning destination, which was frequently the stables. There he would indulge in another silent act of love, communing with Mephistopheles.

It was the morning after the visit of Mr McGloam. The British Museum Egyptologist had left Tawcester Towers, saying that he would arrange transport within the next week to take the sarcophagus of Pharaoh Sinus Nefertop to his laboratory in London. There it would undergo a sequence of detailed tests to confirm his analysis that it was a genuine antiquity. Once those had been completed, Mr McGloam conceded rather grudgingly that he would attempt a valuation of the item.

His acerbic manner meant that he had departed from Tawcester Towers leaving Blotto and Twinks feeling more derided for having been fooled by the fake artefacts than cheered by the discovery of the sarcophagus.

But doomy feelings never lasted long with Blotto. He had woken the following morning in his customary state of benign and vacuous serenity. The container that was the final resting place of Pharaoh Sinus Nefertop would, he felt absolutely certain, resolve the financial problems of Tawcester Towers. So, after a modest breakfast of porridge, eggs, bacon and devilled kidneys, followed by kedgeree, toast and marmalade, Blotto found his footsteps wending with a certain inevitability towards the garages.

Corky Froggett, the gold buttons on his dark blue uniform gleaming, gave the young master a military salute. Blotto had always regarded this customary greeting as something of a joke, but to Corky it was deadly serious. Though he appreciated the many benefits of his life at Tawcester Towers, deep down the chauffeur felt that civilian life was a poor substitute for being in the Army. Life had been so simple then, with the camaraderie of other men whose sole purpose, like his own, was to kill as many of the enemy as possible. For Corky Froggett the Armistice had come far too early; indeed he would have preferred it never to have come at all. War was his natural milieu and everything else a mild disappointment.

Blotto grinned amiably at his underling and without words went to lean against the garage door, light up a cigarette and watch the ceremony of the Lagonda-cleaning.

As ever the first of the processes was the least refined – the pouring of a bucket of water over the whole vehicle. As Corky raised his pail Blotto waited for the reassuring sploshing sound, followed by dripping on to the garage's cement floor.

But as the contents of the bucket were ejected, something strange happened. Rather than the usual translucent jet striking the Lagonda's bodywork, what came out of the bucket was bright red in colour. It spattered over the black soft-top and the gleaming blue paintwork.

'Toad-in-the-hole!' exclaimed Blotto as he moved forward to the car.

He touched the red fluid and put a finger to his nose to smell it.

There was no doubt. Rather than water, the contents of the bucket had been blood.

# 9

# The Plagues of Corky Froggett

Needless to say, not a single red or white corpuscle was allowed to remain on the Lagonda's gleaming surface. Corky Froggett spent the best part of the day ensuring that. He also removed every trace of blood from the garage floor and the offending bucket. Indeed many a murderer trying to clean up the scene of his crime would have envied the thoroughness of Corky's skills.

At the end of the day Blotto rejoined the chauffeur to discuss what had happened.

'It's a bit of a rum baba, wouldn't you say, Corky?'

'Certainly is, milord.'

'I mean, you didn't have a mouse squeak of a notion you were going to find blood in the bucket, did you?'

'Never occurred to me, milord. Not in a million years.'

'So that would rule out the possibility that you smiggled the stuff in yourself?'

Corky Froggett looked deeply affronted. 'Certainly would, milord.'

'No, I didn't mean you kind of did it on purpose. It's just that I've heard of boddos doing the most fozzly things when they weren't aware of them.'

'Are you suggesting I am not compost mentis, milord?

'No, no, not at all, Corky. It's just Twinks was telling me

the other day about some poor foreign pineapple called Fried I think it was . . . and he apparently has some crack-noodled theory that our minds sometimes make us do things and we don't have a blind bezonger of an idea why we're doing them.'

'I can assure you, milord, that I always know exactly why I'm doing everything I do.'

'Yes, yes, I'm sure you do. But with this blood it just seems such a banana-shaped thing to happen, I feel there ought to be some explanation for it.'

'Well, I don't know what the explanation is,' said Corky, still rather grumpy.

'No, no. Whole thing just seems so off the table, that's all. I mean, I suppose the other explanation is that some thimble-jiggler swopped the contents of the old bucket while you weren't watching.'

'I am never not watching, milord.'

'So there wasn't a moment when some four-faced filcher could have slipped into the garage after you'd got all your globbins out and done the swop?'

'No, milord.' Though this was asserted with a good deal of vigour, it was not in fact true. Corky Froggett had been conducting a minor dalliance with one of the Tawcester Towers kitchen maids and she had had a brief moment of freedom that morning before clearing up the family's breakfast. Taking the opportunity to visit the garage, she had joined Corky in the upstairs part for a brief, though mutually satisfying, encounter. But the chauffeur wasn't about to mention that to the young master.

Blotto shook his head in bewilderment. 'Well, it just is a real peculiosity,' he said. A new idea lumbered slowly into his brain. 'Unless, of course, the contents of the bucket were changed by magic . . . ?'

'I don't believe in magic,' said Corky Froggett stiffly.

* * *

49

Amongst the many actions that Blotto's brain was incapable of performing was brooding. Nor was it much good at fretting, agonising or regretting. All of which were very pleasant inabilities to have. As a result, he thought no more about the strange baptism of his Lagonda in blood. He omitted to mention the incident to his sister. In fact, he completely forgot about it and woke the next morning in his customary state of serene benignity. The October sunlight filtering through his bedroom windows echoed his cheery mood.

Blotto breakfasted much as on the previous day, putting away large portions of porridge, eggs, bacon and devilled kidneys. By way of variety he followed that not with kedgeree but with kippers. And he rounded the meal off again with toast and marmalade.

Then he strolled down towards the Tawcester Towers garages where, exactly as on the previous day – or indeed any other day you cared to mention – he found Corky Froggett's cleaning equipment laid out in readiness for the great ceremony of Lagonda-cleaning. The chauffeur once again greeted him with a salute. Blotto once again leaned against the garage door and lit a cigarette.

This morning's bucket contained no unwelcome surprises, though, before dousing the Lagonda, Corky did inspect its contents with some caution. Despite asserting that he didn't believe in magic, he still had the haunted look of a man who feared that the water might transform itself into blood before his very eyes.

But his anxiety was misplaced. The water from the bucket soaked the Lagonda in a very satisfactory manner, enabling the chauffeur to move in with his chamois leathers and brushes and polishes to bring the exterior of the vehicle to the impeccably high standard that he demanded of it. As he went through the time-honoured ritual, Corky Froggett's manner relaxed – or at least relaxed as far as he ever allowed anything, even the smallest bristle of his moustache, to relax.

The chauffeur completed his final double-check that no mote of dust had infiltrated the perfection of his cleaning, then turned and again saluted the young master. Blotto predictably enough said, 'Nice work, Corky,' and started his customary peregrination towards the stables.

But then he changed his mind. Looking around at the splendid autumnal scene, he announced, 'You know, it's such a bellbuzzer of a day I think I'll take the Lag out for a bit of a whizzle.'

'Very good, milord. I take it you mean you will drive yourself?'

'You're bong on the nose there, Corky.' Not noticing the slight disappointment on his chauffeur's face, Blotto went on, 'I'll open up the spoffing throttle and leave every other road-user in my wake! It's just the day for the Lag to show her pedigree. She's such a breathsapper she'll turn every eye on the King's thoroughfare. She really is the lark's larynx.' It was rarely that Blotto waxed so eloquent, and of course the only other two subjects on which he would wax were Mephistopheles and his cricket bat. 'I can't wait to uncage the power of her chargers!'

'Very good, milord,' said Corky Froggett. And he opened the driver's side door for the young master.

As he did so, something small and green jumped out of the car's interior onto his shoulder. It was followed by more small green things springing towards him. So many that he had to hold up his hands to ward them off.

'Great galumphing goatherds!' cried Blotto. 'What in the name of Denzil are those?'

'Frogs, milord,' replied Corky Froggett.


The chauffeur spent much of the remainder of that day removing every trace of amphibian infestation from the leather upholstery of the Lagonda. Blotto spent much of the remainder of that day hunting on Mephistopheles. As a result he completely forgot about the frogs. Nor did he mention them to Twinks.

The next morning, after his customary breakfast (varied only by the introduction of smoked haddock and poached egg rather than kedgeree or kippers), he wended his way back to the garages. As expected, Corky Froggett had the tools of his trade laid out prior to the cleaning of the Lagonda. But the chauffeur himself was behaving in an uncharacteristic manner.

One thing one could always say about Corky Froggett was that he knew how to keep still. Hours of standing on sentry duty, peering out into no-man's-land in the hope of seeing some stray Boche he could shoot, had taught him the habit of immobility. And in his everyday life he strenuously avoided gratuitous motion. Below stairs he was sometimes even nicknamed 'The Statue'.

It was therefore with considerable surprise that when Blotto entered the garage he found his chauffeur virtually writhing. The man seemed to be in considerable discomfort, twitching his limbs about and scratching at his body with a vigour that threatened to unsettle the perfect creases of his uniform.

'What's the bizzbuzz, Corky? What in the name of Wilberforce has got into you?'

'I'll tell you what's got into me, milord – or at least into my uniform. A whole army of these bloody little perishers!'

Blotto did not recognise the object, held between thumb and forefinger, which the chauffeur proffered for his scrutiny. It was about the size of a seed and very close inspection revealed it to be some kind of legged insect.

'What's that when it's got its spats on?'

'A "chat",' replied Corky, using the Army slang word.

'A "chat"?' echoed a bewildered Blotto.

'A louse, milord.'

'Ah.' No wonder Blotto didn't recognise the thing. People of his class did not encounter lice. Like tripe, dripping and Cockney accents, they were reserved for the lower orders.

'I got used to the little buggers while I was in the trenches and managed to stop scratching, but this lot I've got in my uniform . . . blimey, are they giving me some gyp!' He scratched violently to emphasise his point.

'But where have the little pinkers come from?' asked Blotto.

'That,' said Corky Froggett vindictively, 'is what I'd like to know.'


After breakfast the next morning (smoked salmon after the bacon and eggs) Blotto returned to the garage. Corky Froggett had dealt with his infestation of lice – or, to be more accurate, overnight his friendly kitchen maid had done that (among other things) for him.

But the moment they opened the door of the Lagonda, chauffeur and young master were immediately assailed from the interior by a buzzing swarm of huge horseflies, which homed in on their faces and stung them mercilessly.

As he batted the assailants away with both hands, Blotto shouted, 'I've had it up to my ear lobes with all this! I'm going to ask Twinks to unravel the rigging!'

# 10

# Twinks Makes Sense of Things

'Don't you remember anything from reading the Bible?' asked Twinks.

'No,' said Blotto, who was above all things honest.

'Didn't you have religious education classes at Eton?'

'I think we probably did,' he replied judiciously, 'but I sort of didn't notice them.' Again this was true. Much of Blotto's education had passed by in a blur, beaks yattering away while he dreamed of being on the cricket field.

'Religion has never meant much to you, has it, Blotters?'

'No,' he agreed. Then, by way of explanation, 'Well, like you, I am Church of England, after all. So it shouldn't mean much to us, should it?'

Twinks nodded. 'True.'

Brother and sister were snug over mugs of cocoa in her boudoir. He had chronicled the strange events that had been happening to Corky Froggett and Twinks had instantly seen a pattern in them. Clearly, from what she had said, it had something to do with the Bible, and Blotto waited with every ear open for her to tell him what.

'It's the Plagues of Egypt,' Twinks announced.

'Oh?'

'Have you ever heard of them?'

'No.'

'Well, Blotto me old backbrush, it's all there in the book of Exodus.'

'Is it?'

'Oh yes. You see, the Pharaoh had enslaved the People of Israel.'

'Had he, by Denzil? What a stencher! Was this recently?'

'No, it was at the time of Moses.'

'Ah.'

'Which is a long time ago.'

'Right.'

'In Egypt.'

'Tickey-tockey.'

'You see, Blotters, the People of Israel were keen to get away from Egypt.'

'Well, you can understand that, can't you?'

'What do you mean?'

'Well, it's abroad, isn't it? I mean, anyone with their head screwed on the right way round would rather be in England, wouldn't they?'

'The People of Israel didn't want to be in England.'

'Didn't they? Well, that's a rum baba. Where did they want to be?'

'Israel.'

'How very peculiar.'

'They were being enslaved, remember? By the Pharaoh?'

Blotto nodded as the recollection came back to him. 'Good ticket.'

'So you see the People of Israel had a sort of contest with the Pharaoh's priests.'

'What, all the People of Israel?'

'No, just Moses really.'

'Ah.'

'And he had Aaron.'

'You mean he wore a wig?'

'No, not "hair on". "Aaron". Aaron was Moses's brother and he was a priest.'

'Right. On the same page now, Twinks.'

'And Aaron had this kind of contest with the Pharaoh's sorcerers. He did sort of magic tricks.'

'What, like that poor pineapple who came to one of my birthday parties in the nursery and produced billiard balls out of my ear?' It was a childhood memory that had made a deep impression on Blotto. He had spent some weeks afterwards poking matchsticks into his ears in the hope of producing more billiard balls.

'That kind of thing,' said Twinks judiciously, 'but maybe a bit more sophisticated. What Aaron did was to summon up the Plagues of Egypt, in the hope that the Pharaoh'd get so vinegared off that he'd let the People of Israel go home.'

Blotto nodded slowly. He was getting a bit lost. 'But what's all this to do with that poor old greengage Corky Froggett?'

'I was getting to that.'

'Well, shift your shimmy, me old box of tooth powder.'

It wasn't often that Twinks got annoyed by her brother, but that remark did cause a minor tightening of her beautiful lips. She enjoyed telling stories at her own pace. 'The first Plague that Aaron summoned up was the Plague of Blood.'

'And how did that work?'

'Aaron turned the waters of the Nile to blood.'

'Did he, by Denzil?'

'All the fish died.'

'Well, they would, wouldn't they?'

'And there was a terrible stink.'

'I'm sure there was.'

'But then Pharaoh's sorcerers showed they could turn water into blood too. So Aaron summoned up another Plague.'

'And what was it this time?

56

'The Plague of Frogs. Do you see the pattern emerging, Blotters?'

'No,' her brother admitted.

'The entire land of Egypt was overrun by frogs. But the Pharaoh's sorcerers also made frogs appear.'

'There must have been a lot of frogs about the shop,' said Blotto. And he then made one of his rare attempts at a joke. 'Like living in Paris – her-her.'

Twinks chose to ignore that. 'And when all the frogs were killed and gathered up in piles, there was another great stink.'

'Well, there would be.'

'And the next two Plagues Aaron summoned up were the Plague of Lice and the Plague of Flies.'

'Boddo had a nasty imagination, didn't he?'

'Maybe. But you do see the pattern now, don't you, Blotters?'

'No.'

'Well, think.' Her brother's brow furrowed as he tried to follow her instruction. 'You just told me what had happened to Corky, didn't you?'

'Yes.' But Blotto still sounded bewildered.

'First, the water in his bucket changed to blood . . .'

'Mm . . .'

'Just as in the Plague of Blood. Then the Lagonda was filled with frogs . . . just as in the Plague of Frogs. Then Corky became infested with lice . . . just as in the Plague of Lice. Then when he opened the car door, you were attacked by flies . . . just as in . . . ?'

She waited. Blotto looked puzzled. Then, slowly a wide beam irradiated his impossibly handsome face. 'The Plague of Flies!' he announced triumphantly.

'Splendissimo! You're bong on the nose there, Blotto me old grandfather clock! Corky Froggett is being visited by the Plagues of Egypt!'

'Poor old thimble,' said Blotto. 'What a murdy thing for him to have to go through.'

'He hasn't said anything about there being a sequence, has he?'

'Sorry, not on the same page?'

'Does Corky realise that he's being visited by the Plagues of Egypt?'

'No, I'm sure he doesn't. I can't imagine that he's ever read the Bible. Do you think we should tell him?'

'Not yet.'

'But I'd have thought the poor old pineapple would be relieved to hear that it's all over.'

'It's not all over!' Twinks announced dramatically.

'Sorry? What do you mean? Have I got the wrong end of the sink plunger?'

'You certainly have, Blotters. There were more Plagues of Egypt.'

'How many more?'

'Ten in all. Corky isn't even halfway through.'

'Poor old thimble. What else is on the bill of fare for him?'

'After the Plague of Flies comes the Plague of Murrain . . .'

'And what's a Murrain when it's got its jim-jams on?'

'It's a pestilence.'

'Oh?'

'Like a plague.'

'The Plague of Plague then?'

'Sort of. It came upon the Egyptians' cattle, horses, asses, camels, oxen and sheep.'

'Toad-in-the-hole! Bit beyond the barbed wire to take it out on the animals. What came next?'

'The Plague of Boils.'

'Yuk.'

'Then the Plague of Hail, the Plague of Locusts, the Plague of Darkness . . .'

'Darkness as in night?'

'Yes, Blotters, except it happened during the daytime. For three days.'

'Well, I'll be jugged like a hare!'

'And finally,' concluded Twinks in awestruck tones, 'came the Plague of the Death of the Firstborn.'

'Firstborn what?' asked Blotto anxiously.

'Firstborn child.'

His expression cleared. 'Oh well, that'll all be tickey-tockey then.'

'Why?'

'Corky doesn't have any children. So none of them can die, can they?'

Twinks didn't look convinced. 'I'm not sure how Plagues work exactly. Maybe for people who don't have children something else has to die or be destroyed instead.'

'Like what?'

'Well, is there anything in Corky Froggett's life that he loves as much as another person might love a child?'

Blotto thought for a moment. Then his hand shot up to his mouth, as all the colour drained out of his face. 'Great Wilberforce!' he said. 'The Lagonda!'


Brother and sister went together down to the garages to see Corky Froggett. Despite his customary bluff military manner, it was clear that recent happenings had unsettled him.

Blotto immediately went across to his precious Lagonda, inspecting it for damage. He even got in the driving seat and pressed the self-starter. The engine emitted its normal powerful purr, the contented sound of a lion who has just dined on a couple of tasty Thomson's gazelles. To Blotto's relief, all was fine. The Plague of the Death of the Firstborn had yet to strike the Lagonda.

He turned anxiously to Corky Froggett. 'Has there been anything else? Any more murdy doings?'

'Well, milord, there has been one odd thing.' The chauffeur led them to the back of the garage. There, at the foot of the wall in neat rows, lay the tiny corpses of rats and mice.

'The Plague of Murrain,' Twinks whispered to Blotto.

'Plague of what?' Blotto whispered back.

'Murrain.'

'Ah,' said Blotto, as if he knew what it meant.

'Corky,' asked Twinks, 'have you any idea what's causing all these nasty events to happen?'

'No, milady.'

'Well, in fact,' said Blotto, 'it's the Pl—' He saw the deterrent look in his sister's eye. Clearly she wanted to keep the chauffeur in ignorance of the pattern of afflictions – at least for the time being. 'It's the Pl ... it's the Pl ... It's the Plughole! Yes, it's the absolute Plughole of bad luck for you to be stuck in.' He was rather pleased with the dexterous way he'd improvised his way out of trouble.

'Don't you worry, milord,' said Corky Froggett doughtily. 'My only aim in life is to serve you and your family. And if discharging that duty involves a little suffering ... well, it's suffering that I welcome, milord.'

'You're a grade A foundation stone, Corky.'

'Thank you, milord. Anyway, the way I look at this latest affliction is this. These garages have been riddled with vermin for a long time, and whatever's happening, it seems to have sorted them out.'

'Yes.' Twinks looked at him appraisingly. 'And you're feeling all right, are you?'

'Never better, milady. Once I'd got the lice out of my uniform, everything was back in fine working order.'

'Hm.' She was thoughtful. 'Of course in the Bible there's no mention of rats and mice ...'

'I beg your pardon, milady?'

'The Murrain.' Corky Froggett didn't look any less puzzled as she went on, 'It affected the Egyptians' cattle, horses, asses, camels, oxen and sheep.'

There was a long silence while Blotto took in her words. Then alarm flashed across his perfect visage. 'Horses?' he cried. 'Great spangled spiders! Mephistopheles!' And he rushed like a madman towards the stables to check on what – given that, in common with the chauffeur, he didn't have any children – might be regarded as his firstborn.

Corky Froggett looked shyly at Twinks. He was rarely alone with the young mistress and he never felt quite at ease with her. Part of the reason for this was that, like every man whom she encountered – whatever their age – he was more than a little in love with her. Also, as a person of infinite practical skills but few intellectual accomplishments, he was in awe of her mighty brain.

'Do you have any idea, milady,' he asked humbly, 'what the hell's going on?'

'Something pretty fumacious,' said Twinks. There was no point in sugaring the pill for Corky. 'I think you're being possessed.'

'But I always have been, milady.'

'Sorry? Not on the same page?'

'I mean, milady, I have always been a mere possession of the Lyminster family, a good, a chattel. I have never asked for more. It is a great honour for me to serve all of you, milady.'

'Yes, I'm afraid you've rather got the wrong end of the oily dipstick, Corky. I meant that you have been possessed by an evil force.'

'Not the Lyminster family?' asked a rather confused chauffeur.

'No, not the Lyminster family.'

'Then by who?' he demanded ungrammatically.

But before Twinks could tell him, Blotto returned, his whole body expressing huge relief. 'All tickey-tockey in the stables,' he announced. 'Mephistopheles in zing-zing condition. Same goes for all the other nags too.'

'Good ticket,' said Twinks.

'And by chance I met that boddo who runs the Home Farm and he said there were no problems with the cattle, asses, camels, oxen and sheep. Though he did give me a rather funny look when I asked about them.'

'Why?'

'Well, he said we hadn't got any camels.'

'No, Blotters, we haven't.'

'Right. Best to be sure, though. That's why I asked. So, anyway, Twinks, it looks as if it's only the rats and mice who've been affected by the Moron.'

'Murrain.'

'Right.'

'Excuse me, milady,' the chauffeur interposed diffidently. 'You were about to tell me what I've been possessed by.'

'You're bong on the nose there, Corky. So I was.' She thought for a moment. 'But I think it's information that'll keep.'

'Very good, milady,' said Corky Froggett, though he couldn't quite exclude a note of disappointment from his voice.

As brother and sister walked away from the stables, Blotto asked urgently, 'Do you mean you've got a bat-squeak of an idea what's going on?'

'Yes, I'm afraid I have. And it's the explanation, Blotto me old sock suspender, for what's been happening to Corky.'

'Right. So what is it? Come on, uncage the ferrets, Twinks me old Swiss bun.'

'I think,' she announced dramatically, 'that Corky has brought upon himself the Curse of Pharaoh Sinus Nefertop!'

'Broken biscuits!' said Blotto.

'And if we don't find a way of stopping this sequence of events, he's going to have to go through the Plagues of Boils, Hail, Locusts, Darkness and . . .' She paused for effect.

'The Death of the spoffing Firstborn,' her brother supplied. And he looked back with deep fretfulness towards his Lagonda.

'Exactly, Blotto me old butter knife.'

## 11

# A Visit to St Raphael's

In the hope that no further unpleasantnesses would happen to Corky Froggett that day, Twinks announced to her brother that they needed to take a trip to Oxford.

'Oxford? Why Oxford?'

'Because there resides the one person who can possibly get us out of our current treacle tin.'

'Tickey-tockey,' said Blotto, equable as ever.

It was nearly six o'clock by the time the Lagonda drew up outside the gates of St Raphael's College. The porter in his lodge looked very sniffily at them. Twinks knew it wasn't her brother the man objected to. St Raphael's was an all-male enclave. The sight of a woman on its premises was almost unprecedented. And though her beauty and winsome charms could melt most masculine hearts, that organ inside the porter was made of particularly durable stuff.

Unswayed by his look of unwelcome, Twinks announced, 'We have come to see Professor Erasmus Holofernes.'

'I think not, madam,' said the porter.

'I think so.'

'Professor Holofernes does not have visitors.' The porter looked up at the clock on the wall of the lodge. 'Particularly not at this time of the evening. It is the Professor's invariable practice, having worked in his rooms all day, to go to the Senior Common Room for drinks on the dot of six o'clock, prior to dining in Hall.'

'Well, this evening,' said Twinks, 'he is going to change his invariable practice and see us instead.'

'I think not, madam.'

'It's "milady",' said Twinks frostily.

'Then I think not, milady.'

'Very well.' In a gesture reminiscent of the Dowager Duchess, she gathered her silver mink coat around her. 'Come along, Blotto. We're going to find the Senior Common Room.'

'Tickey-tockey.'

'I'm sorry, milady . . . sir . . .'

'He's "milord" too,' said Twinks.

'I'm afraid I cannot possibly allow you to . . .'

But the porter's words fell only on to the night air. By the time he had extricated himself from behind his counter and emerged from the lodge, Twinks, with Blotto in her wake, was already halfway across the quadrangle, following the trickle of begowned academics making their way to the S.C.R.

The gown in front of her passed through a heavy oak door. Gesturing to her brother to hold it open for her, Twinks strode into the room.

The conversation – mostly about such idle topics as abelian and tauberian mathematical theorems, Ricardian economics and etymological cruces in Thucydides – was stopped as if by the pressing of a switch. Speechless dons gazed open-mouthed at the almost unprecedented phenomenon of a woman in the Senior Common Room of St Raphael's College, Oxford.

(The 'almost' was added to the word 'unprecedented' because in fact on two occasions women had breached the ramparts of that male institution. It had not been visited by its Catholic founder Queen Mary, but her sister Queen Elizabeth I had attended a Protestant service at St Raphael's when she was in Oxford to found Jesus College. The other occasion was in the early nineteenth century when a dissolute undergraduate smuggled a local washerwoman into his room for the purposes of fornication. Following the customs of the time, his fate was rustication and hers was mastication by wild dogs.)

So the appearance of Twinks that evening in the Senior Common Room was little short of sensational. Amongst the assembled academics bushy eyebrows rose, jaws dropped revealing yellowed teeth, nervous tics danced across wrinkled features, and not a few pairs of glasses steamed up.

Apparently unaware of the reactions she was causing, Twinks looked coolly round the open-mouthed dons until she saw the one she was looking for. 'Ah, Razzy,' she said. 'I need to talk to you.'

'Of course,' replied the delighted academic. 'Come up to my room.'

And under the still-gaping stare of his colleagues, Professor Erasmus Holofernes led his visitors out of the Senior Common Room.


Blotto supposed that there must be furniture somewhere in the Professor's room, but he couldn't see any of it. Every surface was so crammed with books, letters, folders, files and loose extraneous papers that it was hard to know what lay underneath. Also amidst the strata of documentation lay plates of half-eaten meals and cups full of congealed coffee, whose antiquity could only be guessed at.

But Twinks seemed to know her way around and could locate furniture under the chaos. She sat down atop a teetering pile of dossiers, which somehow bore her thistledown weight. Her brother, being very considerably bulkier, was gingerly in his approach to securing a solid support, but found a perch that didn't wobble too threateningly. Erasmus Holofernes, most of whose adult life had been spent in that space, had homed in instinctively to what must have been a chair behind what must have been a desk.

Blotto didn't know – and Twinks hadn't told him – much detail about the Professor's work. From his room in St Raphael's Holofernes ran a massive information network. His own knowledge was extensive, but he was also in touch with academics all around the world. So, when a question arose beyond the range of his own expertise, the Professor knew exactly the right person to contact for the answer. He occasionally used the telephone – and he was the only don in the college to have a personal instrument in his room – but more frequently he made his enquiries by letter. The extent of his correspondence was so voluminous that the St Raphael's porter employed a boy whose only task was carrying the outgoing and incoming mail between the lodge and Holofernes's room. And his filing system for all this paper was, to put it at its mildest, idiosyncratic (though he could always within seconds lay his hand on any document he required).

In spite of the disorder he inhabited, the Professor proved to be the soul of hospitality. Before leaving the Senior Common Room, he had given instructions to the St Raphael's college butler to supply him and his guests with the same menu that was being served in Hall downstairs. With the same wines, which were of an excellence that one would have expected from the cellar of an Oxford college.

So, after the Professor had reiterated how pleased he was

to see Twinks and toasted her pulchritude in pre-prandial champagne, he turned his attention to her brother.

'Very pleased to meet you at last,' he announced in his dry, rather excitable voice.

'Beezer to meet you too,' said Blotto.

'It is a great pleasure to add your name to my list.'

'Sorry, not on the same page. List of what?'

'Great intellects, Blotto.'

'Oh?' He had never before heard those three words used in the same sentence.

But before Blotto could remonstrate, Professor Erasmus Holofernes was already continuing, 'Most of the great intellects of the world I have met only through correspondence, but there are still many who have been in this very room and sat on the very chair on which you are now sitting.'

'Oh, so it is a chair?' said Blotto with considerable relief. 'Hoopee-doopee.'

'And I must confess that I am a little jealous of you.'

'Toad-in-the-hole, Prof! Why should you be jealous of me?'

'Because, Blotto, I have often prided myself on having the most remarkable intellect in the known world . . .'

'Well, I'm sure if you say you have then you must have, me old pineapple.'

'No. I fear when it comes to direct competition I must bow down and acknowledge you my superior.'

'Don't talk such toffee,' said Blotto, always embarrassed by compliments and rather confused by this particular one.

'But it must be so,' the Professor insisted.

'Well, erm . . .'

'Why, if it is not so, does your beautiful and brilliant sister work with you?'

This was the obvious cue for another 'Well, erm . . .', so Blotto supplied it.

'Not only work with you, but *prefer* to work with you than with me?'

'Now that's not quite fair, Razzy,' Twinks interposed.

'It may not be fair, but it is true. Stop me if you know any of this, Blotto, but your sister and I were first brought together by Scotland Yard.'

'Well, I didn't know that bit, but you just keep on uncaging a few more ferrets and when I hear something that does tickle the old memory glands I'll let you know.'

'Very well. Now Scotland Yard contact me when they are baffled about a case. Which is most of the time. Scotland Yard live in a perpetual state of bafflement. And normally I can help them out from my research.' He gestured to the mountains, valleys, glaciers and foothills of paper that lay around him. 'Anyway, there was a case a few years back – a minor royal's illegitimate son had disappeared and for once my research resources proved inadequate.'

'A very rare occurrence, Blotto,' his sister pointed out, 'as you will discover when you get to know Razzy better.'

The Professor preened himself at the compliment, running fingers through his unruly hair. At that moment a discreet knock on the door announced the arrival of the college butler with the soup course. Once they had balanced their bowls on precarious piles of papers and were sipping away at the rather excellent consommé à la tortue, Holofernes continued, 'Well, the solution to my problem turned out to be your sister. She, you see, had the specialised knowledge that I lacked. She knew the aristocracy. She knew exactly how people of your breeding work. In no time, working together, we had found the missing minor royal's illegitimate son.'

Twinks giggled at the recollection. 'Yes, it was quite a complex case, wasn't it? I'll never forget the cross-dressing bishop.'

'Complex it was maybe, Twinks, but we still solved it in

69

double-quick time. And that's because I was working with you. Well, Blotto, since that time I have had many more requests from Scotland Yard for assistance and in most cases I've been able to oblige. But my efficiency is never so great as when I am working with your sister.'

'Good ticket,' said Blotto.

'And yet, though very often I ask her to come and help me out, very rarely is she available for such service.'

'Well, you know,' Twinks said in her defence, 'a gel does have a rather splendissimo social life to keep up – hunt balls, all that kind of rombooley – so it's sometimes hard to—'

'This is all nonsense, Twinks,' said the Professor brusquely. 'You told me that the reason you couldn't spare time to work with me was that you were busy with other investigations, *on which you were working with your brother.*'

'Oh, yes, well there is a smidgeonette of truth in that, Razzy.'

'So,' Professor Erasmus Holofernes concluded triumphantly, 'that must mean that, rather than working with me, you would rather work with someone whose intellect is more impressive than my own – in other words, your brother!'

Twinks found herself resorting to one of Blotto's 'Well, erm . . .'s.

The Professor turned to face Blotto. 'So I am intrigued by you, of course. For me to have sitting in my room one of the greatest intellects in the world is . . . as you can imagine . . . a very exciting moment.'

'Good ticket,' said Blotto a trifle nervously.

'So tell me . . . is your intellect the product of a very fine education or is it innate?'

'In eight what?' asked Blotto.

'Please don't be frivolous, Blotto.'

'I wasn't being frivolous. I was just asking a straight question and—'

But Holofernes was not about to be interrupted. 'I have been doing some work on the nature of genius, which I will soon be publishing, and I am intrigued by the origins of the phenomenon. In your case do you think it's congenital?'

Blotto blushed. Talking about 'genitals' might be all right in the locker room after a good game of cricket, but it didn't quite tick the clock when there was a lady present. Fortunately the awkwardness of the moment was diffused by the appearance of the college butler with the fish course, *sole de Douvres à la meunière*, which he filleted for them.

If Blotto had hoped that this interruption would divert the Professor from his line of investigation he was out of luck. As soon as the college butler had left the room, Holofernes went on, 'Tell me – were your special qualities recognised early, Blotto? At school did your teachers hail you as a genius?'

At last – a question that was easy to answer. 'No,' said Blotto firmly.

Holofernes nodded. 'It's often the case. Few teachers have the capacity to recognise the truly exceptional. Mind you, in my case once they did see the light, once they realised the huge disparity between my results and those of the rest of the class, there were occasions when I was put in another room, so that I was not forced to work at the same pace as the rest of my classmates.'

'Yes, that happened to me quite a lot too,' said Blotto.

'The reason I'm so interested,' the Professor continued, 'is in comparing my own experiences with yours. Being a genius is not without its drawbacks, particularly when one is growing up and at school. Blotto, did you ever feel that your unusual level of intelligence put a barrier between you and your classmates?'

71

'No,' he was able to reply quite truthfully.

'Was jealousy ever expressed of your intellectual prowess?'

Another easy one. 'No.'

'Might I also ask, Blotto – and I speak as someone who also grew up with an extremely gifted sister – whether there was ever any rivalry between you and Twinks?'

He looked puzzled. 'Rivalry? Why should there ever be rivalry? When we were younger we liked different things. In the nursery I had lead soldiers, she had dolls. Then I had cricket and she had ponies. I suppose,' Blotto recollected judiciously, 'the only place where there was any rivalry was on the tennis court. I mean, obviously I'm bigger and stronger than Twinks, but she's got an absolute whizz-bang of a first service and—'

'No, no,' the Professor interrupted. 'I understand all that, but I was talking about intellectual rivalry. Was there ever any intellectual rivalry between you and your sister?'

'Great Wilberforce, no!'

'Why not?'

'Because, Professor, Twinks has got such a grade A brainbox that various international museums have asked her to donate it to them when she finally tumbles off the trailer ... whereas I ... well, I've often been told that if some stencher snaffled a brain cell out of my cranium, then I'd just have to manage on the one.'

'You mean you're not a genius?' asked Erasmus Holofernes, aghast.

'I'm so far from being a genius,' Blotto replied with serene self-knowledge, 'that the beaks at Eton, who marked our work with Greek letters – you know, *alpha plus*, *beta double plus* and so on – said I was the first pupil for whom they'd had to go down to *omega minus*.'

'Oh,' said a bewildered Professor Erasmus Holofernes.

'But,' said Twinks loyally, 'he is very good at cricket.'

72

'Ah,' said a still-bewildered Professor Erasmus Holofernes.

'Not only good at cricket, but good also at biffing any lumps of toadspawn who get in our way when we're on one of our adventures. Blotto can defeat hordes of stenchers with nothing more than a cricket bat in his hand. He doesn't know the meaning of the word fear.'

Her brother beamed and explained to the Professor, 'There are quite a lot of other words whose meanings I don't know either.'

Holofernes still looked troubled. 'But I can't understand, Twinks, how someone who does not have a mighty intellect can help you in that subtle business of deduction and ratiocination . . .' (another word of which Blotto didn't know the meaning) '. . . whereby a crime is solved.'

'I do all that in my head, Razzy . . .'

'Yes, my sister really is the lark's larynx when it comes to solving crimes,' Blotto contributed.

'. . . but not all crimes can be solved – as you solve yours – without leaving a room,' Twinks went on. 'Often we have to travel on cases and when we do, more than once Blotto's saved my chitterlings. In a clammy corner, he's the absolute top of the milk.'

These expressions of mutual admiration seemed to convince Professor Erasmus Holofernes that the siblings did form a viable pair of investigators. So, after another interruption from the college butler as he brought in their three individual grouse with all the trimmings, he took a long swallow of the excellent college claret and asked, 'So, Twinks my dear, what is the problem that has brought you here to me?'

# 12

# Professor Holofernes Brings his Brain to Bear

There was a long silence after Blotto and Twinks – well, mostly Twinks, actually – had finished their narration. Holofernes took another slow swallow of his claret before announcing, 'You have got yourselves into a very serious situation here.'

'We were rather afraid we might have done,' said Twinks.

'Thought it was probably a bit of a gluepot,' admitted Blotto.

'Presumably, Razzy, you do know the odd factette about Egyptology . . . ?' asked Twinks.

'I know about everything!' replied Professor Erasmus Holofernes. 'I am in correspondence with all of the major Egyptologists of the world.' He gestured to one specific area of the landscape of paper that lay around him. 'There I have all of their detailed findings.'

'But I am right, aren't I,' ventured Twinks, 'in assuming that what's been happening to Corky Froggett does mirror the Plagues of Egypt?'

'You are right. Certainly you are right. But that parallel does raise problems of its own.'

'What kind of problems?'

The Professor ran a frustrated hand across his face, snagging on the tufts of hair he'd missed when shaving. 'The first problem is one of timing.'

'In what way?'

'Well, let us make another assumption ... that the Plagues which have been visited on your chauffeur have been visited on him because he has violated the sacred peace of Pharaoh Sinus Nefertop.'

'You think that is the reason?'

'Why, Twinks? Don't you?'

'That was my first thought, but I'd feel better to have it confirmed by you, Razzy.'

'I am sure it is a reasonable assumption for us to make at this stage of our investigations,' said the Professor judiciously.

'Rein in the roans for a moment!' Blotto interrupted. 'Are you saying all these murdy things have been happening to Corky simply because he lifted the lid off that sarcophy-flipmadoodle?'

'Well, that does seem the most likely explanation,' said Twinks, 'given what was written on the sarcophagus. You know, the Curse?'

'Yes.' Blotto nodded thoughtfully.

'Why?' asked Holofernes. 'Hadn't you considered the possibility of a connection between the two events?'

'No,' admitted Blotto, honest as ever.

The Professor nodded thoughtfully. He was clearly going to have to rethink his theories about the heredity of genius. The existence of Blotto had cast doubt on all of his recent conclusions.

'You said there was a problemette about timing,' Twinks prompted.

'Yes,' the Professor concurred. 'You see, the biblical story of the Plagues of Egypt concerns Moses.' Twinks nodded.

'And Moses was reckoned by current research to have been born around 1525 BC. The common view is that the Pharaoh with whom Moses was described as being in conflict with in the Book of Genesis was Rameses, called "The Great". His dates were approximately 1303 BC to 1213 BC.'

A glaze had spread over Blotto's eyes. It was like being back in a history lesson at Eton while some beak droned on about the causes of the War of the Austrian Succession. As they had done so often then, his thoughts drifted to daring deeds on the cricket field.

Fortunately his sister was more attentive. 'So what you're saying, Razzy, is that for the sarcophagus to have on it a curse related to the biblical Plagues of Egypt, it must date from after Moses's departure from Egypt with the Children of Israel?'

Professor Erasmus Holofernes nodded vigorously. It was such a pleasure to be in the company of an intellect comparable to his own. Pity about the brother, though.

'I don't see why that's a problem, though,' Twinks went on. 'It would put the date of the sarcophagus firmly within the period of the New Kingdom, probably in the Nineteenth or Twentieth Dynasty, when Egypt was at its most powerful.'

Blotto had never before been aware of his sister's likeness to a history beak. So he let his mind drift back to memories of carrying his bat through an Eton and Harrow match of long ago, until serendipitously there arrived another interruption in the form of the arrival of their bread-and-butter pudding.

But that didn't put Holofernes off his stride. As soon as the door had closed behind the college butler, he continued. 'The problem is that, had the sarcophagus come from a much earlier dynasty, of which records are much sketchier, I would not be worried about the unfamiliarity of the name of Pharaoh Sinus Nefertop. But details of the pharaohs of the New Kingdom – and their dates – are pretty well known, and I have never heard a reference to one called Pharaoh Sinus Nefertop.'

Disappointment dulled the azure of Twinks's eyes, as her hopes for a quick solution to the Tawcester Towers financial crisis were threatened. 'Are you saying, Razzy, that the sarcophagus is a fake?'

'Well . . .'

'Mr McGloam, the expert from the British Museum, is convinced it's genuine.'

'I would not wish to challenge his opinion. A nasty little Scottish bounder by all accounts, but he certainly knows his Egyptology.' He sighed. 'I'm afraid it's difficult for me, without having actually *seen* the sarcophagus, to pass judgement on its authenticity.'

'But there's no doubt about the authenticity of the unpleasant things that have been happening to our chauffeur.'

'No, Twinks, I take that point as well.' Holofernes tapped his hair-tufted chin thoughtfully. 'It'll be boils next, won't it?'

'What will be boils?' asked Blotto, emerging from his trance.

'The next Plague of Egypt. The Plague of Boils. So you keep an eye on your chauffeur chappie for any signs of boils.'

'Tickey-tockey,' said Blotto. Then a thought came to him. 'What happens if he's got boils where I can't see them?'

'I beg your pardon?'

'Well, I mean, Corky's always kitted out in his uniform, so the only bits of him I can normally see are his head and his hands – and not even his hands when he's driving because he wears gloves. So if he gets a boil on his face or the back of his neck or his hands . . . well, it's all creamy eclair. But if the poor pineapple gets a boil on another part of his anatomy ... I mean, on the kind of places that boddos get boils ... like on his ... or on his ... or ... Well, how'm I going to find out about that?'

'You ask him.'

'Ah,' said Blotto, grateful as ever for illumination. 'Good ticket.'

'Anyway, Razzy,' said Twinks, 'we need you to lace up your thinking boots. It seems to me a guinea to a groat that Corky Froggett's upset the spirit of Pharaoh Sinus Nefertop, and we need to get the poor thimble off the gaff before something really murdy happens to him.'

'I can understand that.'

'Because after the Plague of Boils he's still got Hail, Locusts, Darkness and then ... the Death of the Firstborn.'

'Which might,' said Blotto in sepulchral tones, 'affect my Lagonda.'

'We must save Corky from all that,' said Twinks.

'Of course you must,' the Professor agreed. 'And, at the first sign of Mr Froggett developing a boil, however small, I am relying on you to telephone me immediately.'

'Fair biddles, Razzy. Of course I will.'

At that point, after a respectful knock on the door, the college butler entered with their savoury of oysters wrapped in bacon, commonly known as 'angels on horseback' (except they weren't really commonly known, because common people never got them). He enquired whether the Professor wished to join the other dons in the S.C.R. for port and brandy or if he would like that too served in his room. Holofernes chose the second option, and the college butler departed.

'So, Razzy,' said Twinks, looking at him with sunny confidence, 'what do we do?'

'Hm.' He scratched through his wild and thinning hair. 'It's a conundrum.'

'But how do we solve the conundrum?'

'I don't know.'

Twinks looked aghast. Never before had she heard those words uttered by Professor Erasmus Holofernes. 'You don't know?'

'I do not.'

'But . . . but . . . but . . .' It was rarely that Twinks looked lost for words. The expression the shock brought to her face did not, in her brother's opinion, suit her.

'I'm going to have to do a lot of research,' announced the Professor. 'When I've finished I will write to you with my conclusions.'

And Blotto and Twinks had to be content with that. Still they enjoyed the Saint Raphael's port and brandy.

## 13

# Murmurs of Revolution

'This is appalling!' said the Dowager Duchess. 'It shouldn't be allowed!'

They were in the Blue Morning Room. Twinks had quickly finished the newspaper article to which her mother was referring. Blotto, never quite so quick on the reading front (he had been working his way through *The Hand of Fu Manchu* for some five years and hadn't quite reached the end), was still deep in the text.

The offending item had been published in that week's edition of the *Tawcestershire Gazette*. Normally such a rag would never have been allowed near the Dowager Duchess but, given the contents, the Tawcester Towers butler Grimshaw had felt it should be brought to her attention. The article was written by Alfred Sprockett and appeared to represent his manifesto for the forthcoming election.

It was pretty combustible stuff. Twinks could see why it would have given the Dowager Duchess the hump. The ideas were very much those that Sprockett had outlined at his rally in Tawsford Town Hall, but of course Twinks's mother had never heard such thoughts expressed. Such thoughts were never expressed in polite society. Her shock was understandable.

To take a few sentences at random, the article put forward the view that: 'The wealth of this country should be distributed equally to every single citizen'; 'Inherited money is money stained with the blood and sweat of serfdom'; 'Honesty is a quality to be found, not in the expensive perfumes of the landed classes, but in the sweat of working men'; 'The revolution that will put an end to aristocratic privilege and provide justice for the poor cannot be far away.'

These broad precepts were not calculated to appeal to the likes of the Dowager Duchess, but she would have liked his polemic even less the more specific it became. The final paragraph must have been a red rag to anyone in whose veins blue blood flowed, and particularly one in whom it had flowed for so many generations.

'Inequality rules all over the country, but nowhere is it more blatantly on display than here in Tawcestershire. The gap between the wealth of the richest in our county and that of the honest men and women who break sweat to till its soil is offensive to all right-thinking individuals. And on our very doorstep stands a mighty symbol of this great injustice – Tawcester Towers. Built by money stolen from the poor, built on land stolen from the poor, maintained by the sweat of the exploited poor, Tawcester Towers represents everything that is wrong with this country. Its huge estate is arrogantly lorded over by a family who do not think it necessary to pay their bills, regardless of the hardship this may cause to local suppliers and shopkeepers who have kept up their productivity by the sweat of their brows. In the new dawn – a dawn that is not now far away – places like Tawcester Towers will still exist, certainly, but they will exist in a new and egalitarian form. They will not be inhabited by idle aristocrats, concerned only with killing animals and battening off the sweat of working men. It is the working men themselves who will walk through the long corridors and sleep in the feather beds of Tawcester Towers. Justice will be done, privilege will be ended and the bloated aristocrats who have for too long lived off the fat of the land will finally have to get jobs and live off the sweat of their brows.'

'How,' the Dowager Duchess demanded of her daughter, 'does he know that we don't pay our bills?'

'Presumably, Mater, the shopkeepers tell him,' said Twinks.

'Huh,' her mother snorted. 'Whatever happened to loyalty?'

'I think,' Twinks offered cautiously, 'the contemporary view might be that loyalty is a two-way process. And if we don't show loyalty to the shopkeepers they might feel justified in not showing any loyalty to us.'

'But of course we're loyal to them. We continue to buy their produce, don't we?'

'Yes, Mater, but we don't continue to pay them for it.'

'Fiddlesticks! A mere detail.' The Dowager Duchess looked at the copy of the *Tawcestershire Gazette* that Blotto was reading as if it had been scraped off the boot of someone who'd just walked through a stockyard. 'Surely,' she bellowed, 'there's a law against the newspapers publishing such seditious nonsense?'

'Apparently not,' said Twinks.

'Then one must be introduced immediately,' announced her mother. 'Loofah must be sent up to the House of Lords straight away to make the necessary arrangements.' Her older son, the current Duke of Tawcester, was rarely required to put in an appearance at the legislative heart of the country, but this was a matter of urgency.

'I fear he may not be successful,' said Twinks gently.

'Why ever not?' demanded the Dowager Duchess. 'After all, who's running this country?'

'Not the House of Lords.'

'Well, they should be.'

'The country is run by the House of Commons . . .'

'What absolute tosh!'

'And we currently have a Labour government.'

'Which gives people the right to disseminate revolutionary rubbish like that?' The Dowager Duchess pointed again at the newspaper for emphasis.

'The expression of almost all political opinions is entirely legal,' her daughter informed her.

'Well, that's ridiculous! Plebs don't have any opinions worth expressing. Everyone knows that. Next thing they'll be letting Socialists talk on the radio!' The Dowager Duchess grunted out a laugh at the incongruity of the idea.

'They already do, Mater.'

'WHAT!!!'

'Yes, they're allowed to read out their manifestos.'

'Disgusting!'

'And there's a new invention called television, which—'

'Television? Such an ugly word. What does it do?'

'It enables people not only to speak, as they do on the radio, but also to be *seen* while they're speaking.'

'What an appalling idea! And are you suggesting that Socialists might be allowed to be seen on this newfangled device?'

'I think it can only be a matter of time, Mater.'

With another baleful look at the *Tawcestershire Gazette*, the Dowager Duchess said, 'I think it's absolutely characteristic of the lack of sensitivity of the lower classes that an article like this should be written at a time when Tawcester Towers is suffering a financial crisis.'

Twinks did no more than nod. She knew that at such moments it was unwise to engage in detailed conversation with her mother.

'On which matter,' the Dowager Duchess went on, 'when is our financial crisis going to be sorted? When is Rupert the Egyptologist's sarcophagus going to be sold?'

It was not the moment to mention Corky Froggett's sufferings or their visit to Professor Erasmus Holofernes, so Twinks just said, 'Mr McGloam, the expert from the British Museum, hopes the transportation of the artefact can be achieved within the next week.'

'Well, tell him to get on with it! That sarcophagus needs to be sold as soon as possible – and for as much money as possible!'

'Yes, of course, Mater.'

Blotto looked up from the *Tawcestershire Gazette*, having read as much of the article as his brain could cope with at one sitting (the first paragraph, to be exact). The Dowager Duchess fixed her younger son with a basilisk stare. 'So . . . what do you think about the views of Mr Alfred Sprockett?'

'Well, Mater,' Blotto replied, 'he does seem a bit obsessed by sweat.'

## 14

# The Professor's Verdict

Blotto and Twinks were restless. Until they heard from Professor Erasmus Holofernes there was nothing they could do except drift listlessly around Tawcester Towers. Meanwhile life there went on as usual. The Duke, Loofah, continued trying to impregnate his wife, Sloggo, with something other than a girl. The Dowager Duchess spent a lot of time on the telephone, patronising her friends. Mr Snidely, Mr Crouptickle's acolyte, carried on creating his painstakingly slow – and entirely unproductive – inventory of the house's contents.

No bills got paid and some of the local shopkeepers even had the nerve to threaten withholding credit from the Lyminster family.

While Blotto and Twinks anxiously monitored Corky Froggett for any sign of boils.

It was only two days after their visit to St Raphael's – but it felt a lot longer – when a letter from Professor Erasmus Holofernes finally arrived. Mr Snidely happened to be in the Tawcester Towers hallway when the postman appeared and he took the pile of mail – mostly final demands from local shopkeepers – to the butler in his pantry. On instructions from Twinks, Grimshaw took the letter from Oxford straight to her boudoir and was then despatched to fetch her brother from the stables where he was ruminating gloomily with Mephistopheles.

As soon as they were alone, Twinks tore open the envelope. Long experience of living with Blotto told her that the quickest way of sharing the communication with him would be to read it out loud. Which is exactly what she did.

'"Dear Twinks,"' (Clearly her brother was considered by Holofernes too much of an intellectual lightweight to be included in the address).

'"Since we met I have given much thought to the problem you raised – and have in fact put many other important investigations on hold while I deliberated on the matter. I have consulted, either by correspondence or telephonically, the world's finest Egyptologists and we are all of the same opinion.

'"The situation in which you have found yourself is, as I suspected, an extremely hazardous one. Though none of the experts I contacted had heard of Pharaoh Sinus Nefertop, from the sufferings that have already been visited on your chauffeur there seems little doubt that he did exist, probably as we surmised in the period of the New Kingdom, during the Nineteenth or Twentieth Dynasty. (It is possible, and my panel of Egyptologists are exploring this possibility, that Pharaoh Sinus Nefertop is an alternative appellation for a Pharaoh documented elsewhere under a more recognised name.)

'"There does not seem to be any doubt that the misfortunes of Mr Froggett have come as a direct result of his opening the sarcophagus of Pharaoh Sinus Nefertop. There is a lot of nonsense talked in the sensational press about curses of the Pharaohs, but there have been authenticated records of bizarre happenings following on the desecration of Egyptian tombs. Whether these are the result of magic or can submit to more rational explanation is not a matter that needs to be discussed at this time. The fact is that such events have happened before, though rarely with the kind of elaborate detail which has been visited on Mr Froggett.

'"The curse spelled out in the hieroglyphs on the sarcophagus would seem to support this theory. The words 'Herein lies the great God King Pharaoh Sinus Nefertop, guarded by the spirits of the living dead. Should anyone unauthorised open the sarcophagus he will be visited by the Curse of Pharaoh Sinus Nefertop!' are as unambiguous as they could be.

'"None of the Egyptologists I consulted have heard of another curse being based on the biblical Plagues of Egypt, but the sequence of Mr Froggett's afflictions seem to offer no other viable explanation. If the parallel is maintained he will, as you said, now be facing Boils, Hail, Locusts, Darkness and the Death of the Firstborn. How these will be achieved in Tawcestershire – particularly the Locusts – I do not know, but the powers of evil are infinitely inventive, so I would not advise you to relax your guard.

'"Since I have, at the time of writing this letter, had no telephonic communication from you, I'm assuming that Mr Froggett has not so far succumbed to the Plague of Boils. It is possible that the Plagues being visited on him are at an end, that the spirits guarding the mortal remains of Pharaoh Sinus Nefertop wished merely to deliver a reprimand to the unfortunate man.

'"I do not, however, believe that to be the most likely outcome in this unhappy sequence of events. I would more incline to the view that the spirits are deliberately delaying their next move, to build up the tension for you, to torture Mr Froggett a little more in his anticipation of the next horror."'

'Well, at least we don't have to don our worry boots about that,' said Blotto.

'What do you mean, Blotters me old shaving brush?'

'I mean that Corky doesn't realise there is a sequence. I haven't mentioned it to him because you told me to keep it under the dustbin lid. And I'm sure he's never read the Bible, so he won't be tying up the bows on it himself.'

'Good ticket,' said Twinks before reading on.

'"So it is important that you and your brother maintain your vigilance and keep a lookout for any sign of boils on Mr Froggett. If such a manifestation does appear, I think there is no doubt that the evil spirits will be seeing the Plagues of Egypt through to the end, right up to the Death of the Firstborn – which could of course have a dreadful effect on Mr Froggett."'

'Or on my Lagonda,' Blotto murmured with feeling.

'"I have therefore consulted with my panel of international Egyptologists if there is any way of obviating the curse of Pharaoh Sinus Nefertop. Various solutions have been offered, but the only one which seems to offer the hope of a happy resolution is a rather drastic expedient.

'"The sacrilege of removing the sarcophagus from its destined tomb was clearly very great. And in fact I would be interested to know at some point the fate of your ancestor Rupert the Egyptologist. If he were to have suffered an early death, there might be comparisons to be drawn with the parlous predicament of Mr Froggett."'

'Got a batsqueak of an idea what happened to old Rupert the Egyptologist, Twinks?' asked her brother, sure she'd know the answer.

His confidence was well placed. 'He died in a hunting accident at the age of eighty-four, a good sixty years after his return from Egypt.'

'So that idea's a bit of an empty revolver,' said Blotto.

Twinks nodded and continued to read Holofernes's letter.

'"But that enquiry should perhaps be held over till another time. The matter of immediate urgency is the safety of your chauffeur Mr Froggett. And my panel of Egyptologists are of the opinion that there is only one way that can be secured. There is no guarantee that the actions required will lift the curse, but they have been proved effective in comparable situations.

'"The only way to restore serenity to the troubled soul of Pharaoh Sinus Nefertop – and incidentally save the life of Mr Froggett – is to return his sarcophagus to Egypt, to the tomb from which it was so sacrilegiously snatched. That, Twinks, is your task."'

'Toad-in-the-hole!' said Blotto.

## 15

# The Dowager Duchess Puts Her Foot Down

Things were not going very well in the Blue Morning Room. Having the smugly smiling Mr Crouptickle present did not make the atmosphere any easier.

'What you're suggesting, Twinks, is preposterous,' boomed the Dowager Duchess.

'It's the only solution, Mater. Isn't that right, Blotto?'

'Tickey-tockey. Bong on the nose. No other trail to follow.'

Their mother's granite features hardened to some new compound which might have proved very useful in the laying of arterial roads. 'I sometimes despair of you two. Given the upbringing you have had, there are many details in the proper conduct of life for people like us which you just do not seem to have comprehended.' She turned to Mr Crouptickle. 'There has been no discernible improvement in the financial situation of Tawcester Towers, has there, Crouptickle?'

'No, Your Grace. Rather the reverse, I'm afraid,' he replied with barely disguised glee.

'And has Mr Snidely yet found anything of value in his inventory of the Tawcester Towers contents?'

'I fear not, Your Grace.'

The Dowager Duchess turned back to her embarrassed offspring. 'Which means that we have only one way of rescuing the estate, and that is by the sale of the sarcophagus which Rupert the Egyptologist brought back from his travels.'

'Yes, but, Mater . . .' The glare that his mother focused on him dried up Blotto's words in his mouth.

'And yet,' the Dowager Duchess continued, 'you are now suggesting that we should not proceed with the sale, that instead you should . . .' she struggled with the incongruity of the idea she was about to express '. . . *return the sarcophagus to Egypt*. Did I understand correctly that that was what you are proposing?'

'Yes, Mater,' said Twinks.

'Yes, Mater,' Blotto echoed.

'But why?'

'Because, Mater,' said Twinks, 'there is a curse on the sarcophagus.'

'Poppycock!' snorted the Dowager Duchess. 'There is no such thing as a curse. You've been reading too many sensational novels.'

'I haven't,' Blotto asserted self-righteously. He still hadn't finished *The Hand of Fu Manchu*, after all. And it wasn't that sensational, anyway.

His mother ignored the interruption, steamrollering on. 'On what do you base this fanciful suggestion that there is a curse on the sarcophagus, Twinks? Do you have anything that might count as evidence?'

'Blotto witnessed a sequence of unpleasant things happening to Corky Froggett.'

'To whom?'

'Corky Froggett,' Blotto supplied. 'He's one of our chauffeurs.'

'Oh,' said the Dowager Duchess, genuinely surprised. 'I didn't know that chauffeurs had names.'

'Well, anyway,' Twinks went on, 'some fairly murdy things have been happening to poor old Corky. They match the Plagues of Egypt. First the water in his bucket turned to blood, then—'

'Twinks, Twinks.' The Dowager Duchess raised a hand to silence her daughter. 'Why are you telling me all this?'

'Because, Mater, you asked me to explain why the sarcophagus had to be returned to Egypt.'

'Well, nothing you have said has provided even a modicum of explanation.'

'But Corky Froggett's suffering,' Twinks insisted. 'And he's going to suffer even more. He's only been visited by five of the Plagues of Egypt so far. There are another five to go, concluding with the Death of the Firstborn. And if Corky starts to get boils, then we're really up to our earlobes in glue. So we must—'

Another imperious maternal hand was raised and Twinks was silenced. 'I am deeply shocked by your attitude,' said her mother. 'You are proposing to put the entire financial future of Tawcester Towers at risk, and the reason for doing it is to stop the sufferings of a *chauffeur*.' Never before had so much withering contempt been loaded on to a single word.

'Yes, that's right, Mater. We—'

'This is what I mean about the two of you not having taken on board any of the lessons of your upbringing. This person to whom you are referring is a *chauffeur*. A member of the plebeian classes. Lyminsters do not change the course of their lives to attend to the needs of *chauffeurs*. We look after our own, and even then only in special circumstances. The welfare of *chauffeurs* is not our concern. They work for us and get paid for their services.'

Mr Crouptickle felt that he had to interpose, 'Except, Your Grace, they don't actually get paid at the moment.

92

The Tawcester Towers wage bill has not been paid for the past three months and—'

'That is irrelevant to my argument!' the Dowager Duchess pronounced. 'The fact is that we Lyminsters have a proud tradition of ignoring the needs of those who work for us. Our rights to do so were enshrined in law under the feudal system – and I'm still not convinced that the ending of that system was a good idea. The law may have changed, but our attitudes certainly have not.' She gestured to the man of business by her side. 'I mean, I'm as likely to care about *his* welfare as I am about a chauffeur's. Such people just are not relevant to people like us, Twinks.'

Mr Crouptickle smiled, apparently inured to that kind of insult. Twinks found herself wondering what went on inside the man's head. Was he affected by the patronising treatment he received? What was his real attitude to his aristocratic employers? Might he be sympathetic to the anarchic notions of someone like Alfred Sprockett? Was the man of business nurturing some master plan for class revenge?

'So let me make this absolutely clear,' said the Dowager Duchess in a tone of conclusion. 'As soon as we get a valuation of the sarcophagus from the British Museum expert, we are going to sell the thing for as much bally money as we can get for it. And, Blotto and Twinks, I categorically forbid you to attempt to take it back to Egypt!'


Both the siblings were restless as they sat over cocoa in Twinks's boudoir.

'Well, the Mater laid down the law like a Turkish carpet,' said Blotto.

'Didn't she just?'

'So a quick pongle over to Egypt's off the menu.'

Twinks sighed 'I suppose it is.'

'What do you mean – *suppose*? The Mater's told us we can't go. That's all there is to it.'

'Is it, though?'

'What?'

'"All there is to it". I've a feeling there might be another fish on the line.'

'What fish?'

'Well, on the one hand we have the fact that the Mater tells us we can't go, so we don't go . . .'

'Ye-es,' Blotto agreed cautiously, so far managing to keep up with his sister's reasoning.

'And on the other hand we have the possibility that, even though the Mater's told us we can't go, we go anyway.'

Blotto was thunderstruck. 'Well, I'll be snickered, Twinks. You do come up with some goods. Are you suggesting we should go directly against the Mater's instructions?'

'Yes.'

Blotto was lost for words. The proposed course of action was unthinkable. From the nursery onwards one rule had obtained at Tawcester Towers: Blotto and Twinks never failed to follow their mother's instructions.

'What's the worst she could do?' asked Twinks, sounding more nonchalant than she actually felt.

Blotto remained silent, contemplating the many worsts that their mother could do. Though not normally very hot on the imagination front, on this occasion his mind came up with an immediate plethora of distressing and painful possibilities.

Something similar must have been passing through Twinks's finely tuned brain, because she sounded even less certain as she said, 'Well, maybe it won't come to that.'

'You see another route through the woods?'

'Not slap off the counter, no.'

94

'Well, how won't it come to that then, Twinks me old carriage clock?'

'I mean there's still a chance that the assaults on poor old Corky have stopped.'

'Sorry?'

'Razzy might be right on the mustard with what he was saying about the evil spirits biding their time, just toying with us, but on the other hand they might think they've already given Corky enough of a slap on the wrist and pulled their troops back.'

Blotto beamed. 'Do you think that's what's happened?'

Twinks grimaced wryly. 'I'd like to think so, but I'm not convinced. I get the impression that the creatures who're guarding Pharaoh Sinus Nefertop in the Afterlife are a pretty vindictive lot. I don't think we've heard the last of the little stenchers.'

'Hope you're wrong,' said Blotto. 'To have more of that guff going on really would be the flea's armpit. I'll feel in trimmer rig when that spoffing sarcophagus is out of the house. That little slimer Mr McGloam said he should get rid of it within the week, didn't he?'

Twinks nodded.

'And that should put an end to Corky's troubles for good and all.'

'I wonder . . .' To Blotto's surprise Twinks giggled before she went on, 'Of course if McGloam does get the sarcophagus out of the house and up to the British Museum, there's a strong chance that he'll be the next person to open it.'

By his standards, Blotto caught on remarkably quickly to her implication. 'Oh, you mean the Plagues of Egypt will be visited on him instead?'

'Maybe.'

'Beezer wheeze! Serve the little Scottish thimble-jiggler right.' He looked relieved. The end of their ordeal was in sight. 'Just get the sarcophagus out of Tawcester Towers and we'll be rolling on camomile lawns.'

'Grandissimo!' Twinks grinned with something closer to her customary sunny confidence. 'Just so long as Corky doesn't show the smallest twingle of a boil developing . . . Have you checked this morning whether he's still off the doctor's list?'

'Erm . . .'

Twinks had known her brother for a long time and could read him like the books that he so rarely read. 'Blotto, you have been checking with him regularly about the boils, haven't you?'

'Well, erm . . .'

She immediately – and correctly – identified this as a no. 'But you great crumb-bag! You promised you would! When did you last run Corky through the question machine?'

'Erk . . .'

'Oh, for the love of strawberries, Blotters! You mean you haven't even asked him once?'

'I have looked,' said Blotto miserably.

'"Looked"? What do you mean – "looked"?'

'Well, each time I've toddled down to watch him clean the Lag, I've looked at his hands and face and he certainly hasn't got any boils on them.'

'But you haven't quizzed him about the rest of his body?'

Blotto looked acutely embarrassed as he admitted that he hadn't. 'The thing is, Twinks, you don't know what it's like being a chappo. Oh, it's all right for you girls. I know, when you cosy up with your chummettes you talk about everything . . .' he blushed a deeper red '. . . even things to do with your bodies. But it's different on the chappier side of fence. I mean, when a bunch of boddos like me get together – you know, even with the muffin-toasters you've been at school with . . . well, you talk about cricket, you talk about hunting, you can talk about wine if you like, or cars. But it's well outside the rule book to talk about anything that *matters*.'

'So,' asked his sister coolly, 'you would regard boils as things that matter – which they certainly do in this particular instance – and therefore not talk about them?'

'It's not easy. I'd feel a bit of a clip-clop asking about that kind of thing.'

'Why?'

'Well, it's kind of . . .' Blotto would by now have won first prize in a Brightest Beetroot Competition. 'With chappos . . . you know, it's not quite the thing to ask chappos what goes on . . . under their clothes.'

'"Under their clothes"?'

'Yes, I mean, you know, I mean one doesn't like to refer to things that are . . . sort of . . .'

'Are you talking about bodies, Blotto?'

'Well, yes, I suppose I am.'

'All people have bodies. Even men.'

'Yes, I know, but that doesn't mean you can just, kind of, casually, *talk about them.*'

'Are you telling me, Blotto, that you haven't even mentioned the word "boil" to Corky?'

'Well, no, of course I haven't. I mean, what's he going to think of me – particularly because he's of the oikish classes and I'm . . . Well, it'd be really beyond the barbed wire for me just to pongle up to him casually and say, "Corky, me old squashed fly biscuit, do you by any chance have any boils?"'

'But, Blotto, you know how important whether he's got a boil or not is!'

'Yes, yes, but . . .' He could only repeat feebly, 'You don't know what it's like being a chappo.'

Twinks shook her head in annoyance. 'Do you want *me* to go down to the garages and ask Corky Froggett whether

97

he's got any boils?' The tone of her voice was highly sarcastic. It was a tone that would have shamed any man into swallowing his scruples and going to do what was required of him.

'Yes, please,' said Blotto.


He kept a distance behind her and stood back shamefaced as his sister strode into the garage. Beside the Lagonda the chauffeur stood to attention as if on parade.

'Corky,' asked Twinks, 'do you have any boils?'

'Yes, milady,' replied Corky Froggett.

# 16

# A Question of Lying

'He still doesn't know,' said Twinks as they walked back to the main house.

'Doesn't know what, me old fruitbat?' asked Blotto, still rather red in the face.

'Doesn't know the significance of his boils.'

'Oh?'

'The fact that they're part of a sequence. The fact that everything that's happened to him, from the water turning to blood onwards, has been a visitation of the Plagues of Egypt.'

'Ah. On the same page with you now. You're talking about Corky.'

'Yes,' his sister confirmed.

'Corky doesn't know.'

'You've potted the black there, Blotters.'

'Do you think we should tell him now?'

'No, keep the hood on the hawk for a bit longer.'

'Tickey-tockey.' Blotto was silent. He was still in a state of shock from his sister's suggestion that they might disobey the Dowager Duchess. And he recognised the chain of logic. Twinks had said they'd have to return the sarcophagus to Egypt if Corky Froggett developed a boil.

Corky Froggett had developed a boil, so . . . the implication was unavoidable. He waited for Twinks to speak.

Which she did, just as they were entering the main doors of Tawcester Towers.

'So it looks like it's Egypt for us,' she said ruefully.

'Good ticket,' said Blotto, though he wasn't really feeling that positive about the situation.

'I think we'll have to.' Twinks sounded as unkeen on the idea as he felt.

'The Mater'll be properly vinegared off. I hate to think how she'll react to someone not doing as she's told them to do.'

'Nobody knows,' said Twinks, and her delicate shoulders succumbed to a shudder. 'It's never happened before. And, what's more, I think we're going to have to lie to the Aged P, as well.'

'Lie to her?' echoed an appalled Blotto.

'Yes. Assuming we're going in the Lagonda . . .'

'Which of course we are.' Blotto took a pretty dim view of 'abroad'. Everything he required of life – cricket, hunting, Twinks – was to be found on the doorstep of Tawcester Towers. And foreigners were, generally speaking, a strange array of specimens. Blotto was not unsympathetic to them. He realised their lives were difficult, blighted by the disappointment of slowly discovering that they hadn't been born British, and he thought a lot of them coped with that appalling disadvantage pretty well (certainly better than he would have done, had he experienced the misfortune of being in their brogues). But the unalterable fact remained that foreign countries and foreign people were foreign. No way round that.

As a result, whenever Blotto did have to leave his beloved country, he tried to surround himself with as many things as possible that reminded him of his idyllic life at Tawcester Towers. So travelling to Egypt in the Lagonda would be absolutely essential. And Blotto would make sure that his cricket bat was safely stored in the car. Pity he'd have to leave Mephistopheles behind, but he recognised the impracticality of taking his hunter to the desert.

Then of course he'd have Twinks with him, to dilute the pervasive foreignness. And Corky Froggett would have to come too. Now the Boils had arrived, they'd have to keep the chauffeur safe from Hail and Locusts. He was a bit hazy about the mechanics of how the Plagues worked, but he recognised that the nearer to Egypt they got, the greater might be the likelihood of encountering Locusts.

'But what's this bizz-buzz about lying to the Mater?' Blotto asked Twinks.

'We've got to get the sarcophagus down from the attic,' she explained. 'And that's not like a hanky you can just slip into a reticule. It's the size of a wardrobe and considerably heavier. The whole house is going to know when that's being moved. Which means we need some cover story as to why we're shifting it.'

'So that the Mater doesn't think we're actually taking it to Egypt?'

'Bong on the nose, Blotto. Needn't be a big lie, not one of those murdy black ones. Something more on the greyish side.' She snapped her fingers. 'I know! We'll tell her we've heard from Mr McGloam and he's coming down the day after tomorrow to collect the sarcophagus. She'll swallow that like a trout takes a damsel. To the Mater's mind, the sooner the thing gets to the British Museum, the sooner the process of selling it can begin.'

Blotto shuddered. 'Sorry, Twinks me old butter-pat mould. It's just the thought of . . . lying to the Mater.'

'I know, Blotters.' And his sister looked rather magnificent as she announced, 'But when the sabre rattles it's the old warhorse who snorts.'

'Tickey-tockey,' said Blotto, totally mystified.

# 17

# A Secret Getaway

Moving the sarcophagus of Pharaoh Sinus Nefertop from the Tawcester Towers attics down to the garages was never going to be an easy task, but at least that part of the plan worked fine from the security point of view. The Dowager Duchess was inevitably roused by the sounds and sights of a large number of her domestic staff manhandling the thing down the stairs, with a lot of oohing and aahing about the human-like form painted on its cover. But she readily accepted her daughter's assurance that the reason for all this upheaval was because Mr McGloam from the British Museum was going to collect it in a couple of days' time. Cheered by the prospect of the imminent resolution of the family's financial crisis, the Dowager Duchess put on her stoutest tweeds, picked up her hunting shotgun, whistled for some dogs, and went out to blast a few partridge to oblivion.

Once the sarcophagus had reached the garages, the helpers from among the staff were dismissed and sent back to their usual tasks. None of them must be allowed actually to witness the concealing of Pharaoh Sinus Nefertop in the Lagonda, or there was a serious danger that someone might snitch to the Dowager Duchess.

As a result it was left to Blotto and Corky Froggett to do the deed which, given the fact that the two of them together could hardly shift the sarcophagus off the ground, was not easy. Though both were men at a peak of exceptional fitness, the dead weight was too much for them. But in his garage Corky Froggett had a system of hoists, hooks and wheels which he used for tasks like lifting out and replacing car engines. Once they had managed to get levers under the artefact and lift it sufficiently to get chains round, the task became easier. In spite of the gearing of the hoist, both men had to strain every sinew to lift the sarcophagus up high enough to loom over the car beneath.

An incautious slip at that moment would undoubtedly have sent the dead weight crashing down, in the process reducing Blotto's precious Lagonda to matchwood, but fortunately the danger was circumvented. Twinks had opened the vehicle's secret compartment, which had been created courtesy of the Mafia, and she was about to guide the sarcophagus into its temporary resting place, when she said, 'Can you rein in the roans for a moment there?'

'What, you mean hold the spoffing thing up in mid-air?' asked her brother, bringing all his weight to bear on the chain in his hands. Had Alfred Sprockett been there at that moment he would have been forced to observe that it wasn't only working men who sweated.

'Just for a momentette.'

Master and chauffeur clung on grimly as the potential wrecking ball of a sarcophagus spun around slowly above the precious Lagonda. Twinks put up a hand to steady it and peered at a decorated band just below the rim of the lid. 'There are some more hieroglyphs,' she announced. 'On the side that was against the wall in the attic. Can you two just hang on for a moment?'

Blotto and Corky Froggett weren't sure that they could. The weight was pulling their arms out of their sockets. But they were both too manly to admit any doubt on the matter. 'Tickey-tockey,' said Blotto.

Twinks took a small notebook and silver propelling pencil out of her sequinned reticule and spelled out the words as she wrote them down. 'Anyone who wishes to escape the curse of Pharaoh Sinus Nefertop must first solve the Riddle of the Sphinx. Hm,' she said thoughtfully, 'now, as I remember, the Riddle of the Sphinx was about—'

'Can we put off the word games till we've got this spoffing sarcophagus safely stowed?' demanded Blotto in some desperation.

'Oh, yes, of course we can.' And Twinks guided the artefact into the Lagonda's secret compartment. It fitted remarkably snugly. The space could have been designed to accommodate dead bodies (as indeed it had been).

Blotto and Corky collapsed on the floor in a heap of perspiring exhaustion. Twinks tapped at her perfect teeth with her propelling pencil. 'Now the Riddle of the Sphinx . . .' she mused.

'Is it that one I used to like in the nursery?' gasped Blotto. 'Something about watches and prison guards and . . . I can't remember what else?'

'I think you're referring to the riddle: What is the difference between a jeweller and a jailer?'

'That's the johnnie! I remember it well.'

'So what's the answer?'

'Oh, I don't remember that,' Blotto admitted.

'The answer is: One sells watches and the other watches cells. Come back to you, does it?'

'Oh yes. It always was a buzzbanger. Did you hear that, Corky?'

'Hear what, milord? I'm afraid I was concentrating on trying to get my breath back.'

'Well, it's this riddle, you see. Absolute buzzbanger. Are you ready for it, Corky?'

'Yes, milord.'

'What's the difference between a watch-seller and a prison guard?'

'I have no idea, milord.'

'Well, it's . . . um . . . it's a . . . erm . . .' Blotto looked perplexed. Short-term memory had never been his strong suit. Nor had long-term memory, come to that.

Twinks intervened. 'It's of no importance, Blotto. The riddle we've got to think about is the Riddle of the Sphinx.'

'And do you know what that is?'

'Of course. Which creature walks on four legs in the morning, two in the afternoon, and three legs in the evening?'

Once again Blotto was perplexed. 'Is it a horse that has some kind of nasty accident jumping a barbed wire fence?'

'No, Blotters. It's a man.'

'What's a man?'

'The creature that walks on four legs in the morning, etc.'

'Oh? Why?'

'Because as a baby he goes on all fours, as an adult he goes on two legs and in old age he walks with a stick.'

'Oh.' Blotto looked puzzled. 'He doesn't live very long, though, does he?'

'What do you mean?'

'Well, if he goes from being a baby to being an old man within a single day . . .'

Twinks decided not to pursue this line of conversation. She knew from experience the problems of trying to get her brother to understand metaphors. Instead, she said, 'All that matters in our current treacle tin is that I've just answered the Riddle of the Sphinx and, if what the hieroglyphs on the side of the sarcophagus are telling is the truth, then we have escaped the Curse of Pharaoh Sinus Nefertop.'

'Oh, that'd be beezer,' said Blotto. But he couldn't keep the disappointment out of his voice. Even though it involved 'abroad' (which he'd never been keen on), he had begun to get rather excited by the prospect of going off with Twinks on another daredevil adventure.

There was a silence. Then his sister announced, 'There's only one way to be sure that the curse has been lifted.' She turned to the chauffeur. 'Have you still got boils?'

'Oh yes, milady,' replied Corky Froggett.

'Then Egypt it is, I'm afraid.'

'Egypt?'

'Do you know anything about Egypt, Corky?'

'No, milady.' This was not strictly true. Corky Froggett did know something about Egypt. Only one thing, and it was something he had learnt in the trenches. That Egypt was where dirty postcards came from. But he didn't think that was an appropriate piece of information to pass on to the young mistress.

'I think you'd better tell him,' said Twinks.

Blotto nodded and took up the cue. 'Corky, old man, there's something we'd like you to do for us.'

'Anything, milord,' the chauffeur replied instantly. 'Anything, even to the point of laying down my life for you. In fact, if the matter can be arranged, I would prefer a task which does involve my laying down my life for you.'

'I don't think it'll necessarily come to that,' said Blotto.

Seeing the disappointment in Corky Froggett's eyes, Twinks hastened to inform him that the mission on which they were embarking would be exceedingly hazardous, and the possibility of their being put in mortal danger could by no means be ruled out.

He seemed reassured by this and asked what it was they wanted him to do. 'As I say, anything. I am honoured to regard myself merely as a pawn in the greater game of life which you, my betters, are playing. And if by any chance it does come to a case of my laying down my life for—'

'As I say,' Twinks interrupted, 'the mission on which we're embarked is one of great potential danger.'

'That's the stuff to give the troops,' said a gratified Corky Froggett. 'And might I be allowed, milady, milord, to guess what the nature of that mission is?'

'If you wish to,' said Twinks.

'Why?' said Blotto.

'Well, it seems to me,' the chauffeur replied, 'that there is only one mission on which you could be embarked. And I base this conclusion on recent events that have been observed in this area.'

Assuming that Corky was referring to the recent transportation of the sarcophagus, Blotto said, 'Good ticket. But I'd bet a guinea to a groat you don't know why we're doing it.'

'Why?' demanded the chauffeur. 'Not very difficult to answer that. You only have to listen to the rotter to know why.'

A furrow broke the surface of Twinks's perfect forehead. 'I'm sorry? To which particular "rotter" do you refer?'

'You must know, milady. I refer to the scoundrel who has announced himself as your sworn enemy, whose sole aim in life is the destruction of Tawcester Towers and everyone connected with it.'

Twinks communicated that further elucidation was still required.

'Why, I'm talking about that double-dyed villain who has been poisoning the minds of local people about the Lyminster family. He's saying that your great fortune has all been built up by robbery and the exploitation of the sweat of the brows of working men and women.'

Blotto's bewilderment cleared. It was the word 'sweat' that had provided the clue. 'You're talking about that four-faced filcher Alfred Sprockett.'

'Of course I am, milord. I think it's appalling that such filthy propaganda should be allowed to be uttered. If everyone was equal – which is the appalling idea that sewer rat is banging on about – what a disaster the world would become. It is right that toffs – if you'll pardon the expression, milord, milady – should be in charge and the working man should know his place. I would be more than happy to—'

'The mission is not about Alfred Sprockett,' Twinks tried to interpose.

But Corky Froggett was too carried away to notice the interruption – or the further ones that occurred through his ensuing speech. 'So I will be more than happy to assist you in your mission to destroy that Socialist blackguard. During the recent dust-up with the Hun I learned a wide variety of killing methods. For Alfred Sprockett I would favour garroting with his own tie . . . or perhaps a bayonet slipped under the ribs while he is sleeping . . . or hanging him by his fingernails from the underside of a—'

'Corky, jam a gag in it, for the love of strawberries!'

This bellow from his young master finally brought Corky back to his senses. 'I'm very sorry, milord. Got a bit caught up in myself there.'

'You certainly did, you poor pineapple.'

'But you do still want Alfred Sprockett eliminated, don't you, milord?'

'No, this mission doesn't have a blind bezonger to do with Alfred Sprockett.'

Corky Froggett looked to Twinks. Experience had taught him that she was a better source of complicated explanations than her brother.

'The mission on which we need to embark,' she said quietly, 'involves the three of us travelling to Egypt . . .'

'Very good, milady.'

'. . . in the Lagonda, taking the sarcophagus with us.'

'Very good, milady.'

'Once in Egypt our mission will be to return the sarcophagus to the tomb from which at some point in history it had been stolen.'

'Stolen, eh?' echoed the chauffeur. 'And what kind of lowlife would steal a thing like that?'

'One of our ancestors,' replied Twinks icily.

'Well, I'm sure he had his reasons,' Corky said hastily. 'Reasons which would be far above the intellectual capacity of someone of my background to understand.'

'You are absolutely right there, Corky.'

'Very good, milady. So, if I may recap the orders so far . . . Our mission is to drive in the Lagonda to Egypt, return the sarco . . . whatever you said . . . to its rightful place. And what do we do after that?'

'We return here to Tawcester Towers.'

'Excellent. Instructions received and understood, milady. And may I ask when our mission starts?'

'Before daybreak. As soon as we've all got our bags packed.'

'Very good, milady.' Corky Froggett was completely unruffled by the suddenness of this demand on his time. It was not his place to ask questions. His sole purpose in life was obedience to the young master and the young mistress. And if following their instructions involved the laying down of that life . . . well, all the better so far as he was concerned.


It was just after 2 a.m. when the Lagonda nosed its way down the long drive towards the splendid gates of Tawcester Towers. The garages were far enough distant from the main house for the three to have no worries about their departure being heard, but in case of some insomniac housemaid seeing them go, Blotto kept the headlights off until they had emerged from the estate.

It was hard to tell how the Lagonda was handling on the gravel of the drive. He'd have to wait till he got onto the open road to assess how much the bulk of the sarcophagus was slowing them down. But Blotto had unwittingly carried the bullion from America all the way back to England hidden in the same compartment, so he was well prepared. The Lagonda would probably not have the full raw power which he so relished, but she'd still get them to their destination all right.

The car's top was up against the sharp October air. Inside the vehicle was an atmosphere of suppressed excitement. The three of them – Blotto, Twinks and Corky Froggett – were off on another adventure! 'Larksissimo!' cried Twinks.

Within Blotto's uncomplicated mind the excitement was mixed with two other emotions. First was a sense of security from the knowledge that his faithful cricket bat was safely stowed in one of his valises in the Lagonda's dickey. And second, he had a feeling of guilty devilment. For the first time in their lives he and Twinks were deliberately going against the instructions of the Dowager Duchess.

Hope the old dinosaur's all right, was his fond parting thought as the Lagonda slipped out into the dark, misty lanes of Tawcestershire in the direction of the South Coast.

## 18

# The Dowager Duchess Alone

It was some time before the absence of the two youngest members of the Lyminster dynasty was noticed at Tawcester Towers. Unless she had house guests to patronise, the Dowager Duchess tended to have her first meal of the day brought up to her bedroom rather than risking the danger of having conversation addressed to her in the Breakfast Room.

(She was one of those people who believed that had God intended her to say a civil word to anyone before noon, he would have fitted her body with some kind of gramophonic device for that purpose. Certainly no civil word had ever been said to her husband, the late Duke, in the morning – and very few had been spoken later in the day. Like most people of their class the two had had separate bedrooms from the kick-off. Some conjugation had been required in the early days of their marriage, but once the Lyminster dynasty was possessed of an heir and a spare and a daughter to breed from, such distasteful encounters had been speedily discontinued, to the considerable relief of both parties involved. The relationship between Duke and Duchess had, both found, worked best when they didn't see each other from one day's end to the next, a situation that was quite easy to achieve in a place as large as

Tawcester Towers. Particularly since the Duke spent most of his waking life shooting or hunting on his extensive estates. Husband and wife had been obliged to meet for the occasional formal dinner where they were well enough bred to maintain conversation with house guests in whom they had no interest at all. Otherwise, the less they saw of each other the better. In the view of most of their acquaintance, an ideal marriage.)

So the absence of her son and daughter from the breakfast table was not noticed by the Dowager Duchess. Nor was it much remarked by the domestic staff. They were used to the contents of some chafing dishes being returned untouched to the kitchen when the Breakfast Room was finally cleared.

Besides, the young master and the young mistress led very free lives. Blotto quite frequently took an early morning spin in the Lagonda or a ride on Mephistopheles and lost track of time, only to return ravenous for his lunch. Twinks's movements were equally random. She was quite capable of dropping into the Tawcester Towers library on her way to the Breakfast Room and becoming absorbed in some task like translating *The Odyssey* into Sanskrit, which could fill three or four hours before she noticed the time.

In fact, the only person aware of anyone's absence that morning was the kitchen maid with whom Corky Froggett had been enjoying a dalliance. Having finished clearing the Breakfast Room, she had wandered over to the garages in expectation of a stimulating encounter and found only disappointment. Back in the kitchen she came across a note from Corky, saying that he'd had to go to Egypt. But, given her rather delicate situation in relation to the chauffeur, she didn't think it prudent to mention his absence to any of the other staff.

As a result, it wasn't until the following morning that Blotto's and Twinks's disappearance was registered. The fact that the Lagonda and its chauffeur had also vanished suggested that they might have left on some extended trip.

Grimshaw, the Tawcester Towers butler, brought this conjecture to the Dowager Duchess in the Blue Morning Room.

'What do you suggest I should do, Your Grace?'

'Do we have to do anything?' True to her breeding, the Dowager Duchess had never been sentimental about her children.

'Well, Your Grace, it is very unlike Lord Lyminster to be away from home in the middle of the hunting season.'

'True. Are there any rumours below stairs as to what might have happened?'

'There is a suggestion, Your Grace, that Mr Froggett the chauffeur might have gone to Egypt.' Grimshaw hadn't heard this from the kitchen maid. She had told no one, but the letter Froggett had left for her had been read by all the other kitchen staff before she got to it.

'Does Mr Froggett have family connections in Egypt?'

'Who can say, Your Grace?'

'Then why do you tell me this, Grimshaw?'

'I tell you, Your Grace, because the possibility had occurred to me that Lord Devereux and Lady Honoria might have accompanied him to Egypt.'

'No, they haven't done that,' came the categorical response from the Dowager Duchess.

'Very good, Your Grace.'

'My younger son and daughter did say they wished to go to Egypt, but I told them they couldn't. So they won't have done.'

'Very good, Your Grace.'

And there the matter rested.

* * *

113

It was in the Blue Morning Room later the same day that the Dowager Duchess acceded to Mr Crouptickle's request for an interview.

'What is it?' she asked testily. Nothing could shake her deep patrician loathing for plebeians like accountants and solicitors. 'Why do I need to see you?'

'I thought it would be timely, Your Grace, for me to give you a review of the current state of the Tawcester Towers finances.'

'Why, Crouptickle? Has anything materially changed since you last gave me such a review?'

'Not a great deal, Your Grace. And certainly nothing for the better.'

'Then why are you bothering me?'

'I thought I should inform you, Your Grace, on the results of Mr Snidely's creation of an inventory of the contents of Tawcester Towers.'

'Oh?' For a moment hope shed a small light on the tectonic plates of the Dowager Duchess's features. 'Did he find something valuable?'

Rather than reply to this Mr Crouptickle, looking more than ever like some predatory black insect, said, 'You may have observed that Mr Snidely is no longer working at Tawcester Towers, that he has not been here for the last two days.'

'Why should I observe that? Snidely is not the sort of person I notice. His presence or absence is a matter of complete indifference to me.'

'I merely mention it, Your Grace, because the reason he has left is that his inventory is completed.'

'And?'

'And?' Mr Crouptickle repeated.

'*And*,' said the Dowager Duchess peevishly, 'did he unearth anything of value?'

'No, Your Grace.'

'If that was all the information you had to give me, Crouptickle, why did you need to set up a meeting? You could have sent me a message to that effect.'

'Indeed I could, Your Grace, but there were other matters I wished to discuss with you face to face.'

'What other matters?' To the Dowager Duchess Mr Crouptickle's manner was becoming very close to insolent. He was behaving as if he rather than she were the person in charge of their meeting.

'I will come on to those in due time,' he said smoothly, confirming her impression. 'First I would like to give you a bulletin about the current state of the Tawcester Towers finances.'

'You've told me already that you want to give me a bulletin,' the Dowager Duchess snapped, 'so I don't know why you're making such a fuss about it. By telling me you'll only be doing your job. What else do I pay you for?'

'You don't pay me. That is rather the point, Your Grace. I haven't been paid anything for over six months.'

'A trifle, Crouptickle. You know you'll be paid eventually.'

'Ah, but I don't know that. And in fact I am in a unique position to know how very unlikely I am ever to be paid by you.'

'How dare you!' The Dowager Duchess's steel-grey hair stood up in affront like the bony frill of a triceratops. 'Remember to whom you are talking. Are you suggesting that members of the Lyminster family do not pay their debts?'

'I am not suggesting it, Your Grace, I am stating it. The fortunes of the Lyminsters have always been based on taking what did not belong to them.'

'People have been horsewhipped in this house for saying less!'

'I'm sure they have. But who is going to horsewhip me? The current duke?'

'Don't be ridiculous.' The image of Loofah horse-whipping anyone – or indeed doing anything useful – was too incongruous to bear contemplation.

'Well, since your other children, Your Grace, are absent and since the rest of your staff are so sick of not being paid that they are on the verge of mutiny, I am not too worried about the prospect of my being horsewhipped.'

'If I had one here,' the Dowager Duchess growled, 'I'd take a whip to you myself!'

'Fortunately you don't have one here.' But Mr Crouptickle looked round the Blue Morning Room with some anxiety. He knew she was quite capable of carrying out her threat.

'But the Tawcester Towers staff are loyal,' the Dowager Duchess insisted, a note of bewilderment in her voice.

'I'm afraid loyalty very rarely survives bankruptcy, Your Grace.'

'Bankruptcy?'

'Yes, Your Grace.'

And with the same relish he had demonstrated at an earlier meeting in the Blue Morning Room, Mr Crouptickle proceeded to itemise the full extent of Tawcester Towers' debts. Mr Snidely's inventory had found not a single object of value that was not already mortgaged. The same was true of all the family estates. Most of the staff were on the verge of departure, and no local businesses would extend further credit to anyone with the name of Lyminster.

When he had finished this litany of disaster, Mr Crouptickle was surprised to see a thin smile creep like a fissure across the rocky promontories of the Dowager Duchess's face. 'What you appear not to have realised,' she said with some complacency, 'is that all of these debts will be settled as soon as the sarcophagus found in our attics is sold. Mr McGloam, the expert from the British Museum, is arriving tomorrow morning to collect the artefact.'

116

'Ah, how sad.' Mr Crouptickle steepled together his long thin hands.

'Sad?'

'That you should believe the sarcophagus is still here on the premises.'

'But of course it is. It was moved down from the attic a couple of nights ago and taken to the garages.'

'Where it was loaded into your son's Lagonda, in which he, his sister and the chauffeur known as Mr Froggett then set off to return the sarcophagus to Egypt.'

'But they can't have done that!' spluttered the Dowager Duchess.

'Why not?'

'Because I expressly forbade them to do so.'

Mr Crouptickle smiled pityingly. 'You would not be the first parent, Your Grace, who has been disobeyed by their children.'

'But my case is different. I am the Dowager Duchess of Tawcester.'

The pitying smile transmuted into a less pitying snigger. 'I fear, Your Grace, that in the current circumstances that counts for nothing.'

She looked stunned. 'So if I can't sell the sarcophagus, what else can I do?'

Mr Crouptickle had clearly been waiting for this cue. His response was instantaneous. 'I have had an approach recently from a consortium of businessmen . . .'

'What kind of businessmen?'

'They are involved in the hotel trade, Your Grace.'

'Hotels?' The way the Dowager Duchess reacted to the word, he might as well have said 'sewerage'.

'And they would be prepared to offer a very reasonable price for Tawcester Towers, with all its estates and all its debts, thus enabling you and your family to move

somewhere smaller, with no worries about the main-
tenance costs of such a large—'

'Crouptickle!' the Dowager Duchess thundered. 'If there
is one thing of which I am certain in this life, it is that
Tawcester Towers WILL NEVER BECOME AN HOTEL!'

'But, Your Grace—'

'NEVER! How dare you make such a suggestion? How
dare anyone in my employ display such impertinence!'

'I dare to do it, Your Grace,' said Mr Crouptickle unctu-
ously, 'because I am about to leave your employ.'

'But you can't do that, Crouptickle. You're my man of
business.'

'No longer, Your Grace. As of this moment I am severing
all links with Tawcester Towers.'

'But—'

He rode over her. There was no longer any ambiguity
about the insolence of his manner. 'And I will await the
announcement in my daily newspaper of Your Grace's
bankruptcy – with some pleasure!'

The door to the Blue Morning Room slammed shut
behind Mr Crouptickle, but his effrontery still lingered in
the air.

The Dowager Duchess was in a state of shock. Suddenly
she looked as old as her family history. She breathed
shallowly and with difficulty as if she had just received a
physical blow. And indeed the blows she had experienced
were more hurtful than mere bodily buffeting. Tawcester
Towers was on the verge of bankruptcy. The sarcophagus
whose sale was to restore the Lyminster family fortunes
had been stolen away.

And the perpetrators of that theft were her younger son
and her daughter. Who – and this hurt most of all – had
set out for Egypt expressly against their mother's orders.

A long injured silence obtained in the Blue Morning
Room. The Dowager Duchess's face seemed to be fighting

some strange unwonted agitation. Could it be possible that a tear was about to trickle down those craggy features?

But no. Breeding will out. The blood of Lyminsters who had fought at Crécy was not so easily diluted. With a snort of contempt, the Dowager Duchess of Tawcester picked herself up out of her thronelike chair and went off to murder some more partridge.

# 19

# On the Open Road

The Lagonda's handling didn't feel as sharp as it usually did. Hardly surprising, considering the weight of Pharaoh Sinus Nefertop's sarcophagus. But Blotto, who did most of the driving, was used, from his American experience, to controlling the car with its secret compartment loaded. So they made pretty good time on their travels through Europe.

One of the many things that annoyed him about 'abroad' was the fact that its residents drove on the wrong side of the road. Blotto had encountered a similar illogicality when he'd been in the United States of America. Still, nothing to be done about it. He made a compromise, characteristic of his nationality and breeding, by powering the Lagonda straight down the middle of every road. This did lead to a few bicycles and laden oxcarts being forced into roadside ditches, but Blotto didn't worry about that. The people on the bicycles and oxcarts (who wore berets or lederhosen, according to which country the Lagonda was driving through) seemed mostly to be of plebeian stock. Besides, they were foreign, so one couldn't really get too concerned about them.

The atmosphere inside the Lagonda was decidedly jolly. Twinks sat beside her brother, constantly shouting out

'Larksissimo!' as some new splendour of European landscape was revealed, while in the back of the car Corky Froggett mentally catalogued the kind of dirty postcards he planned to acquire when they got to Egypt. He also, as they entered each new country on their route, gleefully related how many of its nationals he had killed during his time in the military.

Nor did they stint on the way, eating lavish lunches at quaint hostelries and booking in to the best hotels available. Some people of a nit-picking nature might question how, given the parlous state of the Tawcester Towers finances, they could afford these indulgences. The answer was that Twinks always kept a stash of gold sovereigns in her sequinned reticule, ready for just such emergencies. And, anyway, in most parts of Europe everything was a lot cheaper than in England.

As they had found on a previous European trip to Mitteleuropia, crossing borders between countries offered no problems. There was still an appropriate deference among foreigners to the sight of a British passport. And so complex were the dynastic entanglements amongst the aristocracies of Europe that, in whichever country they entered, the Lyminsters usually had influential relatives in place somewhere.

So no pleb of a border guard had the temerity to suggest examining the contents of the Lagonda. And the sarcophagus of Pharaoh Sinus Nefertop passed serenely on its course towards its homeland.

Twinks and her brother had agreed still not to tell Corky Froggett about the Plagues of Egypt, from whose manifestations he had suffered so much. Better that he should not be anxious in anticipation of the next affliction. (Blotto, of all people, knew the truth of the adage that 'ignorance is bliss' – he had lived in bliss for most of his life.) But Twinks did keep asking Corky if he'd still got boils.

121

Receiving on each occasion a reassuring 'Yes, thank you, milady,' she every now and then looked warily up at the sky, anticipating a sudden attack of hail.

Needless to say it was Twinks who had decided the route by which they would travel to Egypt. As well as the other invaluable contents of her sequinned reticule, she kept in there a complete set of the latest road maps of Europe and Baedeker guides to the countries they might travel through. From Calais, where they'd arrived on the ferry from Dover with the Lagonda strapped down on the deck, they had driven through northern France into Germany (where Corky Froggett claimed his highest number of victims). Then into Austria (quite a few) and the Kingdom of Yugoslavia (twelve), on the way to Greece (only two), where they planned to get a ferry from Piraeus to Alexandria.

It was early evening when they booked into the best hotel in Athens. Eschewing the delights of its restaurant, Twinks (who had of course done her homework with the relevant Baedeker guidebook) suggested they should 'go native' and dine in one of the traditional tavernas in the Plaka area of the city. Blotto, who was as hungry as Mephistopheles, thought this was 'a beezer notion', but Corky Froggett, pleading tiredness from their long journey, said he'd have an early night.

Though the evening was temperate and some of the locals were sitting outside, smoking rough cigarettes as they clouded their glasses of ouzo with water, Blotto and Twinks opted to eat inside the taverna for which she had read a recommendation. They were shown to a table with a perfect view of the Acropolis. The moon was nearly full and they could see every detail of the splendid structure.

To Blotto, however, it didn't seem that splendid. 'Do you think we should ask the waiter boddo for another table, Twinks me old boot button?'

'Why?'

'Well, we don't want a view of a building site, do we?'

'That, Blotters, is one of the most famous buildings in the world.'

'Toad-in-the-hole, is it?'

'Have you never heard of the Parthenon?' The question was out of her lips before she realised the folly of asking it.

'No,' said Blotto.

'Athens was one of the greatest cities of the ancient world. It was here that Greek civilisation reached its apogee.'

'Did it, by Denzil?'

The waiter brought a flask of retsina and poured it for them. Blotto took a healthy swallow. As the taste hit him, he said, 'Great galumphing goatherds, what's in that?'

'Resin,' said his sister.

'The boddos out here drink resin?'

'Yes, it's an acquired taste.'

'And not one that I think I wish to acquire.'

'You'll come round to it, Blotters. It grows on you.'

'So does athlete's foot.'

'Try a bit more.'

Wincing, Blotto drained his glass. 'What's the stuff called when it's got its jim-jams on?'

'Retsina. The name's supposed to come from the resin with which the ancient Greeks sealed their amphorae.'

'Four-eye? Who's got four eyes?'

'No, Blotters. An amphora is a distinctively shaped Greek vessel. Made of clay.'

'Well, it can't have been much good.'

'What do you mean?'

'Any vessel made of clay's going to sink, isn't it?'

'Not that kind of vessel, Blotters, not a boat. It's a container, usually for wine.'

'Ah.' Her brother was silent for a moment. 'And it's called an "apogee"?'

'No, it's called an "amphora". An "apogee" is something else.'

'A boat made of wood, that floats?' Blotto hazarded hopefully.

'No. An "apogee" is the highest point of something.'

'Ah.'

'Do you understand?'

'No,' said Blotto, refilling his glass with retsina and downing it in one. 'I'll tell you what seems a bit of a wonky donkey to me . . .'

'What?'

'Well, the old beaks at Eton who used to teach us classics kept going on about the greatness of Greek civilisation and I must say . . . passing my peepers over this place, you know, here in Athens, well, it doesn't seem so spoffing great. More of a run-down shanty town, I'd say.'

'Ah, but the high point of Greek civilisation, Blotters . . .'

'When it reached its amphora, you mean?' asked Blotto, pleased to show off his new word.

'Apogee,' said Twinks. 'And that apogee – or high point – occurred more than two thousand years ago.'

'Did it, by Denzil? What went wrong? How did the poor pineapples end up in such a gluepot?'

Twinks smiled. 'There are as many theories about that, Blotters, as I've got pink camisoles. If you like, I could give you a reading list as long as cricket match of books you could read on the subject.'

'Better not, perhaps, old greengage,' said Blotto, aware that he still had to get to the end of *The Hand of Fu Manchu*. And then he was struck by an extremely rare moment of philosophy. 'It's a bit of a rum baba, isn't it,' he said, his noble brow wrinkling in puzzlement, 'that these ancient Greek boddos should have cranked up their civilisation until it was in absolutely zing-zing form a couple of thousand years ago and then let the whole flipmadoodle go banana-shaped?'

'If you think that's a rum baba,' said Twinks, 'you wait till you get to Egypt.'

'Not on the same page, Twinks me old sock suspender?'

'The Egyptians have an even longer history as a great civilisation. And yet modern Egypt is pretty much of a stretcher case. Same thing happened with Rome. Once the most powerful empire in the world, then it declined and fell. I don't suppose you know Gibbon?'

'Yes, I do,' said Blotto self-righteously.

'Oh?'

'I saw one in a zoo once.'

'That was . . . oh, never mind.' Twinks knew there were some conversations just not worth pursuing with her brother. 'Anyway, Blotters, it seems an inescapable fact of history that all great empires decline and fall.'

'Not all of them.'

'What do you mean?'

'Oh come on, Twinks, tune up the brainbox.' It was very unusual for Blotto's sister to be slower of perception than he was and he couldn't help himself from slightly glorying in such moments. 'Think of the map.'

'What map?'

'Why, the map of whole spoffing world. Think how much of it is painted pink.' Blotto's noble heart swelled with patriotic pride as he went on, 'You say all empires decline and fall, Twinks me old tub of shoe polish, but that's never going to happen to the jolly old British Empire, is it?'

\* \* \*

125

Corky Froggett, when he had said he was going to have an early night, had been guilty of a minor untruth. The reason that he didn't want to join the young master and the young mistress for dinner was not tiredness, but a desire to explore an unfamiliar city with the satisfaction of another desire in mind. Still feeling slightly cheated of the encounter with his kitchen maid that he had been anticipating before their summary departure from Tawcester Towers, he quickly found an area of the city of Athens where there were plenty of young ladies more than willing to accommodate his requirements.

In the same area he also found a purveyor of dirty postcards. Disappointed by their lack of photographic sophistication and clarity, he only bought a few. His recollections from comparative assessments amongst his fellow soldiers in the trenches assured him that the quality of the product in Egypt would be superior. He looked forward to sampling them.

It was as he was returning, in a benign state, towards the hotel that Corky Froggett saw something which rather surprised him. Outside a taverna, sipping ouzo and deep in conversation with a tall man wearing dusty brown clothes and a broad-brimmed leather hat, sat someone he recognised. The man's skeletal frame and black suit left Corky in no doubt about his identity.

It was Mr Snidely, Mr Crouptickle's underling, who only a few days previously had completed his abortive inventory of the contents of Tawcester Towers. Corky Froggett could not for the life of him imagine why the accountant should be in Athens. Or indeed who his companion might be. In his brief awareness of the man's presence at Tawcester Towers, the chauffeur had not regarded Mr Snidely as the kind of person to boast an international range of clients or acquaintances.

It was odd, but then in the course of his long and active life Corky had encountered many things that were odd. Confident that in the shadows of the street he had not been spotted by Mr Snidely, he continued on his way. And as he did, he made a decision.

The young master and the young mistress wouldn't want to know about the doings of oikish characters like Mr Snidely. Besides, if Corky were to raise the matter, they might ask rather too searching questions about how he happened to be out on the streets of the city when he had told them he was going to have an early night.

So he kept the sighting of Mr Snidely to himself.

# 20

# The Land of the Pharaohs

The Lagonda was lashed on to the deck of a ferry in Piraeus and transported painlessly to Alexandria. The journey was not, however, so painless for those who had been travelling in it. Athens had been fairly temperate for early November, but the further south they went, the hotter the weather became. And because of the precipitate way in which they had left Tawcester Towers, only Twinks had thought to pack a summer wardrobe.

So, as they drove from Alexandria to Cairo in the Lagonda with its top down, she sat comfortably in a cotton shift, cooled by the air rushing past. While her brother in his three-piece tweed suit and Corky Froggett in his dark blue chauffeur's uniform both sweated like pigs. People with a less rigid sense of decorum might have taken their jackets off, but neither Blotto nor Corky would have done that in the presence of a lady.

And the chauffeur had the additional discomfort of his unseen boils. Twinks, still hoping that her solving the Riddle of the Sphinx might make the Plagues abate, kept verbally checking with Corky that the boils were still in place. And each time she asked, they were.

'I think,' she announced, 'as soon as we get to Cairo, we must fit you chaps out with some new togs.'

'Yes, I'd feel a lot more cushly in a blazer and flannels,' Blotto admitted. 'And the Old Etonian tie.'

'I'm not sure,' said Twinks, 'that you'll be able to buy an Old Etonian tie in Cairo.'

Her brother laughed. 'Oh come on, me old toenail clipper, there's surely nowhere in the world where you can't buy an Old Etonian tie.'

'Well . . .' said Twinks dubiously.

As well as his British certainty about Old Etonian ties, Blotto maintained his British certainty about the way he drove in Egypt. It was very similar to the way that he had driven through Europe. The drifting sand on either side of the road made going down the middle the only real option. The main difference was that some of the people he forced off the road were on camels. And rather than berets or lederhosen, they wore long white robes.

These Egyptian road-users were at greater risk from the Lagonda than their European counterparts had been. Because of the huge weight of the sarcophagus-laden Lagonda and the amount of sand on the road, there was an ever-present risk of the great car sinking in and becoming immobilised. The only way for them to avoid that hazard was driving the vehicle at maximum speed to maintain its momentum. Which only served to increase the potential danger to everyone else on the road.

After one donkey cart had been missed by a hair's breadth and ended up buried in a roadside dune with its owner's legs waving in the air, Twinks said, 'Hold back the hounds a bit, Blotto. Don't want to sour up the locals.'

'Just showing them who's in charge,' said her brother.

'But we're not in charge.'

He looked shocked. 'You mean this isn't one of the bits of the map that's painted pink?'

'Great Wilberforce, no, Blotters. Egypt isn't part of the British Empire.'

'Oh.' He thought about this for a moment, then he said, 'Well, it spoffing well should be.'

'We still have quite a bit of influence here, though.'

'I should jolly well hope so.'

'Egypt was even a British protectorate for a while.'

'Was it?'

'Yes, you see Egypt's status was as an autonomous vassal state of the Ottoman Empire.'

'Ottoman Empire?'

'Yes, Blotters.'

'What, a whole empire named after one of those footstool things?'

'I think it was the other way round. The footstool things were named after the empire.'

'Toad-in-the-hole!'

'Blotto, would it help if I gave you a short history of modern Egypt?'

Her brother grinned. 'Sweet of you, Twinks me old back collar stud, but no thanks.'

Mercifully, though there were some breathtakingly close calls, nobody was actually killed during the Lagonda's progress from Alexandria to Cairo. And the injuries didn't amount to more than a few sprains and bruises (and those again were only to foreigners). But it was just as well that the English party's arrival in Egypt was not meant to be secret. Though used to the visitations of foreign tourists, the locals could not fail to be aware of this particular invasion – the huge blue car with its three pallid passengers thundering across their desert roads.

Navigating one's way through the great sprawl of Cairo is a challenge even to its residents, but Twinks had done her homework on the most up-to-date Baedeker and guided Blotto seamlessly through the narrow crowded streets and markets to the city's grandest hotel, Shepheard's. She had cabled ahead from Athens to reserve rooms and as soon as brother and sister had given *baksheesh* (or what Blotto, who didn't like foreign words, called 'tips') to the doorman, the receptionist, the porter, the liftman and other uniformed flunkeys they met on the way, they were installed in adjacent suites. There electric fans mercifully stirred the heavy air off the Nile into an inadequate but still welcome breeze.

Needless to say, Twinks had secreted in her sequinned reticule an address book containing contacts for useful people in Cairo (as she had for every major city in the world – and a good few minor ones). After she had settled into her suite, she returned to the hotel's cavernous and opulent lobby to make a couple of pertinent calls from one of the telephone booths. Then she crossed to Reception.

'Good evening, milady,' said the smiling Egyptian behind the counter, who not only spoke immaculate English but had clearly been briefed about his guest's nobility.

'Good evening. I was wondering . . . would it be possible for you to arrange the despatch of a cablegram?'

'Certainly, milady. There will of course be a small matter of a *baksheesh* to expedite the . . .' Twinks tipped him. The receptionist reached under the counter for a brown form. 'If your ladyship would like to fill out the content that you wish to write?'

'Tickey-tockey,' said Twinks.

It was a message she had been wanting to send ever since they'd left Tawcester Towers, but this was the first opportunity she'd had. Ever since she had deciphered the second row of hieroglyphs on Pharaoh Sinus Nefertop's sarcophagus, there was something about them that had been puzzling her. She needed the help of an expert.

On the brown form, with the fountain pen she kept in her sequinned reticule, she wrote in the box provided:

'Thank you for your letter – your advice bong on the nose as ever. Have followed it and are now in Cairo, shortly to return the sarcophagus. One questionette, though ... Hieroglyphs on the other side of it say Curse will be obviated by solving the Riddle of the Sphinx. Any thoughts on this?'

And she filled in the addressee's details as Professor Erasmus Holofernes of St Raphael's College, Oxford. She handed the completed form back to the receptionist. And tipped him again.

# 21

# A Meeting of Experts

Twinks's work on the telephone had produced immediate results. While she and her brother were dining in Shepheard's Hotel's splendid Moorish Dining Room, a uniformed bellboy approached their table with a telephone message. Once he had received *baksheesh*, he handed it across.

'Larkissimo!' said Twinks when she had read the text.

'Grern?' asked her brother who was chewing his way through a rather tough steak.

'After dinner we're going to meet someone useful.'

'Gnar,' said Blotto, still chewing.

'Is there anything else, milady?" asked the bellboy.

'Yes. Could you arrange for our chauffeur to have the car outside the front entrance in . . . half an hour?'

'Of course, milady.' And he held his hand out for further *baksheesh*.

Following the young mistress's instructions, Corky Froggett guided the great Lagonda through the narrow streets of Cairo. In spite of the lateness of the hour, the alleys were still crowded and the brightly lit bazaars open. With the car's top down, the English visitors could smell the mix of spices, roasted meat and other less salubrious aromas. From the cafés and bars they passed emanated Arabic music and the occasional sounds of jazz.

Corky brought the Lagonda to a halt outside another hotel, the Two Pharaohs, of much more recent provenance than Shepheard's. In fact, it looked as if it had only been completed the previous day. There was a lot of new development along the banks of the Nile. After the upheavals of the Great War Cairo seemed to have woken up to the potential for international tourism. Hotels were springing up all over the place.

While Blotto and Twinks went inside the hotel's grand entrance, Corky Froggett stayed in the car, already the object of considerable interest from the street children who flocked around it. He had to maintain extreme vigilance to ensure that no hubcap, leather strap or other detachable part should be detached from the gleaming vehicle. (Though the Lagonda had arrived in Cairo covered in dust from its desert drive, Corky had spent all the time since in the Shepheard's Hotel's garage buffing up the bodywork to meet his customary exacting standards.)

Having given *baksheesh* to the uniformed doorman who directed them through the open door, Blotto and Twinks approached the concierge. Once he had been tipped, he told Twinks where to find the gentleman with whom she had made a rendezvous. He then summoned a uniformed flunkey who, having been tipped, led them through the Two Pharaohs's ostentatious opulence to a terrace built out over the Nile. Elegant tables and chairs were laid out under giant purple umbrellas. At the water's edge was a landing stage, so that guests could embark and disembark from the motor launches and *feluccas* that took them on sightseeing trips. Stars and lights from the far side were reflected in the dark surface of the mighty river. For the first time the day felt almost temperate.

The siblings were led to a linen-covered table at which sat a tall young man wearing the moustache and uniform of a British Army major. He rose immediately at their approach, and tipped the uniformed flunkey. 'Good evening,' he said. 'I'm Major Rollo Tewkes-Prudely. You must be Lady Honoria Lyminster and Lord Devereux Lyminster.'

'Bong on the nose, Rollo,' said Twinks, offering her slender hand to his large outstretched one.

'Welcome to Cairo.'

Blotto saw something he recognised in the Major's eye, something he'd seen so often before that a wave of deep boredom swept through him. All the symptoms were there – the sagging lower jaw, the soft panting sound, the popping eyes, the slight sheen of sweat on the forehead, the total inarticulacy. Yes, there was no doubt about it. Rollo Tewkes-Prudely, like so many before him, had fallen in love with Twinks, instantly and as heavily as a giraffe on an ice rink. He goggled at her like a goldfish with hiccups.

'Thank you. It's a great pleasure for us to be here. And please call me Twinks.'

'Blotto,' said Blotto.

'No, I'm not,' said the Major. 'I've only had a couple.'

'No, my name's Blotto. People call me Blotto.'

'Ah. Right. Anyway, take pews and let's get you something to gargle with. What'll it be?'

As she sat down, Twinks looked across at his glass. 'Is that a dry martini?'

'Certainly is.'

'So they do cocktails here?'

'Certainly do. In this hotel they pride themselves on doing everything just like the Brits and the Yanks do. Haven't been open long, so they don't always get it right, but they give it their best shot.' His eyes were still locked

135

on the azure perfection of hers. 'So is it a martini for you . . . drier than a Saharan sandstorm . . . Lady Honoria?'

'Twinks.'

'Sorry?'

'I said you should call me Twinks.'

'Ah. Righty-ho. Twinks it is. Martini?'

'Do they do a Cobbler's Awl?'

'Sure they do. What's your poison, Blotto?'

'Tell you what'd really bang the bull's-eye. There's something called a St Louis Steamhammer . . .'

Rollo Tewkes-Prudely snapped his fingers and a lurking waiter sidled out of the shadows to take his order (and be tipped). Then the Major sat back and just gazed, mesmerised, at Twinks.

She was used to this. Having grown up being the kind of breathsapper she was, Twinks accepted soupy looks from amorous swains as just an occupational hazard. To tell the truth, she hardly noticed them any more. So she was quite brisk in bringing Rollo Tewkes-Prudely back to his senses. 'I said on the telephone that it was an archaeological matter on which I wanted your advice . . .'

'Yes, yes.' He dragged himself back from the vision of his English stately home with Twinks as its chatelaine and a bevy of flaxen-haired children gambolling at their feet. 'Yes, archaeological – right. Well, nothing out here's a problem on that front. All the johnnies out here who run the archaeological shooting match are French for some reason.'

'Napoleon, perhaps?' suggested Twinks.

'Not with you.'

'It was Napoleon who revived interest in Egyptology as a result of his 1799–1801 expedition here.'

'Was it?' said the Major, his eyes once again glazing over with visions of flaxen-haired children.

Their drinks arrived. Once the waiter had been tipped, they all sipped gratefully. Blotto's cranium felt the afterglow of the pyrotechnic display a St Louis Steam-hammer always set off in there.

Unwillingly, Rollo Tewkes-Prudely refocused his mind on the promising present rather than the glorious future. 'Well, as I say, the French control the whole business, so whatever you want to do, it has to be done through the Frogs. Not that that's a problem. Like everyone else out here, they're as corrupt as hell, so you just have to make sure the right bribe goes to the right person. And the Johnnie you want in this case is a particularly slimy Frog with whom I've had a lot of dealings over the years. His title's Administrator of Archaeology, something like that. He'll get you whatever you need . . . excavation licence, permissions, export licence if there are treasures you want to take back to Blighty . . . so long as you pay his going rate. I can organise an introduction to him for you, easy as pie.'

'It's not actually getting treasures *out* of the country that we're after . . .' Twinks began.

'Whatever it is, the Frog's still your man.'

Twinks decided not to amplify at that point what their real intentions were. Instead she said, 'I mentioned on the telephone about our needing advice from some archaeological experts . . .'

'Don't worry.' Tewkes-Prudely looked at his wristwatch. 'Two of Egypt's finest – well, not that they're Egyptian, of course – will be joining us shortly.'

'Thank you, Rollo,' said Twinks, and she smiled one of her special smiles.

Rollo Tewkes-Prudely was once again instantly submerged in reverie. The first of the flaxen-haired children, he decided, they would call Herbert, after Lord Kitchener.

As Corky Froggett got out of the Lagonda for the fourteenth time to chase off cheeky Arab street boys, he saw someone he recognised going in through the hotel entrance. The man was wearing the same clothes, which made him look like some kind of dusty cowboy. The broad-brimmed leather hat, salty with sweat stains, was unmistakable.

It was Mr Snidely's companion from the café in Athens.

Coincidence, thought Corky Froggett, probably just coincidence. For a moment he felt tempted to mention his sighting to the young master – or more probably the young mistress, who was better at making connections between things.

But then again, he thought, if he did raise the matter there was no way he could avoid giving more detail than he wished to about how he'd spent that evening in Athens.

Probably safer to keep quiet about the whole business.


Rollo Tewkes-Prudely was shaken out of his dream of flaxen-haired children by the approach of a man in dusty brown clothes and a leather hat. He leant across, enveloping himself in Twinks's heady perfume. Resisting the strong temptation to plant a kiss on her oh-so-kissable lips, he murmured, 'Watch out for this cove. Very mercenary, drives a hard bargain.'

Then he rose to greet the man. 'Bengt,' he said. 'May I introduce Lady Honoria Lyminster and Lord Devereux Lyminster? This is Bengt Cøpper.'

The newcomer assessed them through small blue eyes surrounded by tight wrinkles born of squinting at the sun. Twinks felt no romantic attraction in his gaze. He seemed to be valuing her and Blotto, as a cattle farmer might cows at market.

'What will you drink, Bengt?'

'Beer. Stella. Cold.' His English was good; only its sing-song quality revealed his Scandinavian origins.

Another flick of fingers from the Major and the waiter (once he had received his *baksheesh*) scurried off to fetch the order.

The man in dusty brown sat down. 'Bengt,' said Rollo, 'is originally from Norway and he is one of the foremost archaeologists currently in Egypt.'

The man nodded in acknowledgement of this claim, but he seemed in no hurry to initiate conversation. He waited for the Major to continue.

So Rollo Tewkes-Prudely did. 'Lady Honoria and Lord Devereux – who incidentally are known to everyone as Twinks and Blotto . . .' Still the Norwegian said nothing but his blue eyes seemed to question why anyone ever should be given names like that. 'Anyway, they  need assistance on a rather unusual mission and it's one I thought you might be able to help them on, Bengt.'

'I'll help anyone on anything,' said Bengt Cøpper, 'so long as the price is right.'

'Money's no object,' said Twinks.

'No, we—' But a look from his sister stopped Blotto before he completed the sentence. Somehow she'd intuited he was going to say, 'No, we haven't got any.'

'So what is it you want doing?' asked the Norwegian. 'Want me to find you a nice little sarcophagus you can take back to England to display in the Great Hall of your stately home?'

'No, by Denzil!' said Blotto.

'In fact, we want you to help us do the exact opposite of that,' said Twinks.

'Oh?'

And she explained about the depredations of Rupert the Egyptologist. 'Most of the stuff he brought back was fake,' she concluded.

Bengt Cøpper chuckled. 'Yes, there have always been a

139

lot of shysters out here, on the lookout for upper-class Englishmen of very low intelligence.'

Blotto looked puzzled. He had a vague feeling someone was talking about him.

'Anyway,' said Twinks, 'what we want is to return the sarcophagus to the burial ground from which it was taken.'

'Taken? Stolen, I think you mean.'

She shrugged. 'Whatever.'

'And do you know the name of the person whose remains are inside the sarcophagus?'

'Pharaoh Sinus Nefertop,' Twinks announced.

Bengt Cøpper nodded thoughtfully. 'I haven't heard of him, but many of the pharaohs were known by more than one name.'

The waiter arrived with the archaeologist's Stella. Once he had been tipped, he put bottle and glass down on the table and poured. Bengt Cøpper took a long, grateful swallow before asking, 'Do you have any idea what dynasty your Pharaoh might be from?'

'An expert we consulted in England reckoned, from various pieces of corroborating evidence, that the sarcophagus probably dates from the Nineteenth or Twentieth Dynasty.'

'Relatively recent then.' The archaeologist nodded again, before adding with a note of contempt. 'Though I'm not sure how much credence should be placed on the word of an expert who is not in Egypt.'

'The gentleman in question is extremely reliable,' said Twinks coldly.

'Huh.' Bengt Cøpper was again thoughtful. 'So you want to know how much I would charge you to find the relevant burial ground and help you get the sarcophagus reinstalled there?'

'Bong on the nose, Bengt.'

'Hm.' He did some mental calculations, then named a figure.

It was surprisingly less than Twinks had been expecting. From the expression on Rollo Tewkes-Prudely's face it was also less than he had been expecting. The hard bargainer appeared to have gone soft. His charge would easily be covered by the stash of sovereigns in the sequinned reticule, and leave enough for them to drive the unburdened Lagonda back in style to Tawcester Towers.

'What will that include?' asked the Major, more used to the minutiae of this kind of negotiation than the arrivals from England. 'Permissions, excavation licences, hire of local labour?'

'Those will be extra,' said Bengt Cøpper.

Rollo Tewkes-Prudely did a few sums in his head, then announced the total cost of the enterprise. It would eat up almost all of the sovereigns (many now converted into Egyptian pounds) in Twinks's stash – particularly if you took into account all of the tips that would inevitably have to be added to the basic services. She mentally revised the level of lunching they would be enjoying on their return trip through Europe.

'The first thing I will need to do,' said the archaeologist, 'is to see the sarcophagus.'

'Tickey-tockey,' said Twinks.

'Presumably you had to smuggle it in? Or did you just pay the outrageous bribes the customs officials demanded?'

'We smuggled it in – no problems, all creamy eclair.'

'So where is it now?' In their nests of wrinkles, Bengt Cøpper's blue eyes gleamed with excitement. To be introduced to a new rarity is every archaeologist's dream.

'In fact it's in my brother's car, parked directly outside this hotel. Would you like to go and pop your peepers on it?'

'You bet,' said Bengt Cøpper. 'But we should not do it in the open street. You have a driver?'

'Of course,' said Twinks, wondering why the question needed to be asked.

'If he drives down into the hotel's car park, we will be unobserved. I can take a preliminary look at it there.'

'Splendissimo! Let's do it zappity-ping!' Twinks rose to her feet as she spoke. So did Rollo Tewkes-Prudely and Bengt Cøpper. 'Are you coming, Blotters?'

To be quite honest he didn't feel like it. Blotto had been aware of not contributing much to the recent conversation. In fact, he'd been pretty thoroughly edged out of it. He didn't know anything about archaeology, nor did he have any interest in the subject. Why not let his sister deal with the academic and practical aspect of this particular adventure? Then when derring-do was required, that'd be the moment for him to put his oar – or rather his cricket bat – in.

Besides, the waiter had just delivered another round of drinks. And those St Louis Steamhammers had an enchanting way of uncoupling the very tenuous links of logic in his brain. They delivered a very benign muzziness. 'No, I'll sit this one out,' he replied to his sister.

'Probably a good wheeze,' said Rollo Tewkes-Prudely. 'Then there'll be someone here when the other archaeologist arrives.'

'Good ticket,' said Blotto.

'Though,' Rollo continued, almost to himself, 'if Bengt Cøpper's taking the job, there's not going to be much for the other archaeologist to do.'

Then, following the 'ladies first' principle that had been one of the mainstays of his education, he gestured Twinks to lead the way back into the hotel. His eyes were out on stalks as he watched her elegant figure slinking ahead of him. Bengt Cøpper brought up the rear.

* * *

142

Blotto took a long sip from his St Louis Steamhammer, detonating more small comforting explosions in minor parts of his brain. He felt quite relieved to be on his own. And though generally immune to the effects of beauty, he could not help being impressed by the night sky over Cairo.

He still wished he was back at Tawcester Towers, though. Then he could have gone down to the stables and set the world to rights with Mephistopheles. Blotto became lost in the reverie.

'Jolly good evening to you! Waiter Johnnie said I'd find Rollo Tewkes-Prudely at this table.'

Shaken out of his dream, he looked up at the sound to see a galumphing brown-eyed blonde in khaki shirt, trousers and dusty brown boots skitter to a halt in front of him. In spite of the difference in colouring, there was something in the girl's rangy movements and the set of her teeth that reminded him instantly and irresistibly of Mephistopheles.

'Toad-in-the-hole!' said Blotto. 'Good evening.'

# 22

# Christabel

'I'm Blotto,' said Blotto.

'Too many of those, I dare say,' said the girl, pointing mischievously at his St Louis Steamhammer and making the same mistake as Rollo Tewkes-Prudely had.

'No, no, it's my name. And I'm hardly wobbulated at all.'

The girl sat down, as if astride a horse. 'My name's Christabel Whipple.'

'Good ticket,' said Blotto. And then, in a rare moment of perspicuity, he observed, 'You're the other one.'

'Sorry?'

'You're an archaeologist.'

'Give that pony a rosette!' said Christabel, slapping Blotto heartily on his shoulder. 'Yes, I'm an archaeologist. Archaeology is the absolute love of my life. So if you've got any old fossils in your family who need investigating, I'm your lass.' And she laughed. Blotto was transfixed. Even her laugh reminded him of Mephistopheles.

'And I was expecting to meet a chap called Rollo here,' she went on.

'Ah yes. He was here a moment ago, but he just had to pongle off. Be back in two flicks of a fish's tail.'

'Righty-ho. I'll wait.'

'And I'm sure you'd like a drink.' Blotto snapped his fingers for the waiter who manifested himself instantly. 'What's it to be?'

'Lemonade.'

The waiter nodded, waited till he had been tipped, and then dematerialised.

'You off the alkiboodles, Christabel?'

'Pretty much. Except for high days and holidays. Then I've been known to gullet down the champers in large volume. But generally . . . well, it's an occupational hazard . . . the dreaded morning after. Hard to reassemble the pieces of a three-thousand-year-old vase when your fingers are shaking like a cocktail-maker's. Besides the alkiboodles has a devastating effect on my fielding.'

'Fielding? Do you like cricket too?' said Blotto, more pleased than he could say.

'Like it? Love it, Blotto, with a passion. Never was enough cricket at school so far as I was concerned. Went to a convent and nuns aren't that keen, God rot 'em. Also, with their long habits, very difficult to judge lbw, hell for umpires. But I had brothers, so I played with them – and could generally outscore the little wretches. Was once smuggled into a First Class game, dressed as a boy. Scored a double century.'

Blotto hardly dared believe what he was hearing. If Christabel Whipple was as keen on hunting as well as cricket, she'd be the perfect piece of womanflesh. Tentatively he asked her.

'Hunting? Love it, love it. By golly, if there was anything half resembling a fox out in the desert tomorrow, it'd be on with the pink coat, then up and after it like a cheetah on spikes . . . even if I had to ride a jolly old camel!'

A tremor ran through Blotto. He'd never before believed that the perfect woman existed, but now he feared he might have to revise that opinion.

'Anyway, Blotto,' asked Christabel, 'what brings you out to jolly old Cairo?'

'I'm here with my sister.'

'Ah, maybe she's the filly Rollo mentioned. Lady Honoria Somethingorother?'

'Twinks.'

'Lady Honoria Twinks?'

'No, she's called Twinks. Everyone calls my sister Twinks.'

'Ah, righty-ho. Blotto and Twinks.' She didn't speak the names with any hint of criticism. Clearly, like the Lyminsters, she came from the kind of background where it was bad form for nicknames to have any relevance to the person they were attached to.

'Good ticket. What do you get called for short?' asked Blotto, hoping to increase the intimacy between them.

'Christabel,' said Christabel.

'Ah. Tickey-tockey. What are you actually working on out here?'

'I'm with a team digging in the Valley of the Kings.'

'Are you, by Denzil?'

'Anyway, Rollo said your sister Twinks had some archaeological problem and he thought I might be able to help you sort it out.'

'I'm sure you could,' said Blotto, certain by now that she could do absolutely anything she set her mind to. He found himself staring into Christabel Whipple's eyes. The brown pupils had perfect rings of white around them. Again, just like Mephistopheles.

Also, she was as tall as Blotto was. Not something that happened often with the girls he encountered.

A deeper tremor ran through his manly frame. He couldn't identify it, but he felt pretty sure it was a feeling he had not felt before.

* * *

The garage beneath the Two Pharaohs still smelt of fresh cement and was relatively empty. The hotel had not been open long enough to build up a large clientele, but the few cars parked there included a couple of Rolls-Royces, a Daimler, two Hispano-Suizas, a Duesenberg and a Pierce-Arrow roadster. In this exalted company Blotto's Lagonda still managed to look like an aristocrat.

Fortunately there were no hotel staff or chauffeurs around in the garage at that time of the evening, but Bengt Cøpper still took the precaution of locking the gates before he turned his attention to the vehicle which Corky Froggett had just driven in from the street.

There was not a lot of light down there, but Twinks reached into her sequinned reticule and produced an electric torch, elegant in design but with a surprisingly powerful beam. This she directed into the interior of the Lagonda so that Corky could open the car's hidden compartment. The Mafia engineers had done their work well and the floor panels slid back with ease to reveal the painted sarcophagus.

Bengt Cøpper's excitement mounted as the outline was revealed. 'Yes,' he said in a fierce whisper. 'That's the one!'

'You've seen it before?' asked a curious Twinks.

'No, no, of course not. But I have heard rumours of the existence of such an artefact. I just did not expect ever to have the good fortune to behold it with my own eyes.'

Rollo Tewkes-Prudely was also impressed. 'I've seen a lot of this kind of guff out here, but few in such good condition.'

Twinks pointed out the rows of hieroglyphs to Bengt Cøpper. 'I've done sort of rough translations of them.' And she recited her versions.

'Very good,' he said. 'Almost one hundred per cent accurate. How is it that you can read hieroglyphs?'

'Oh, just the kind of thing a girl picks up,' she replied airily.

Rollo's dream took on a new dimension. All those flaxen-haired children were going to be not only beautiful but also incredibly brainy.

'And I've got the name right, haven't I?' asked Twinks.

The archaeologist consulted the hieroglyph and confirmed, 'Pharaoh Sinus Nefertop. Yes, that it right. It is strange I do not know the name. But do not worry. There are reference works I can consult in the Museum of Egyptian Antiquities which will tell me how he was more commonly known.'

'Will those reference works also tell you the location of his tomb?'

'I am sure they will, Twinks,' said Bengt Cøpper with a satisfied smile. 'And now . . .' he stepped into the Lagonda '. . . I am just going to check the sarcophagus's contents.'

'Don't do that!' shrieked Twinks. 'Don't lift the lid!'

The Norwegian looked back at her, a sardonic smile playing around his lips. 'What is this, Twinks? Have you been listening to stories of mummies' curses?'

'Well . . .'

'Do you believe the threat written in the hieroglyphs on the side of the sarcophagus?'

'Yes, I spoffing well do.'

'You should not. Such things were written to deter grave-robbers. They have no potency. As little power as a guard dog with no teeth.'

'But I have seen the power they have,' said Twinks.

'Have you?' asked Bengt Cøpper.

'Have you?' echoed Corky Froggett.

Twinks suddenly realised that she still hadn't explained to the chauffeur the reason for the sequence of uncomfortable events that had afflicted him. And she decided now wasn't the moment to do it. Repeating that she thought the archaeologist would be very unwise to open the sarcophagus, she led Rollo Tewkes-Prudely and Corky Froggett up the stairs that led to the Two Pharaohs' foyer.

When the three of them got back to the table on the terrace, they found Blotto and Christabel Whipple deep in a mutual reverie. Eyes locked, they were testing each other on Test match scores from the previous twenty years. (Though Blotto could not at times even remember his own name, he had remarkable photographic recall for the minutiae of cricket.)

'Oh, Christabel,' said Rollo as they approached, 'I'm so sorry to have dragged you over here. When I didn't hear back after I'd left the message for you at the museum, I went ahead and called another archaeologist Johnnie, and I'm afraid he's agreed to take on the job.'

'Don't worry about it.'

'But I do, old girl,' said Rollo Tewkes-Prudely. 'I'm afraid yours has been a wasted journey.'

'Oh . . .' Christabel Whipple smiled soupily at Blotto. 'I wouldn't say that.'

Then she said she ought to go. In his farewells Blotto informed her about seventeen times that he could be contacted at Shepheard's Hotel. Christabel wrote down her home address, the address of the museum and the site where she was working, along with a list of telephone numbers where he could leave messages. They parted, each more vehement than the other in their assertions that they must meet up again soon. 'I'm working at the Museum of Egyptian Antiquities most of this week,' Christabel kept saying. 'At the Museum of Egyptian Antiquities here in Cairo.'

After Christabel had gone, Rollo Tewkes-Prudely snapped his fingers for the waiter and ordered another round of drinks. Blotto took advantage of the momentary diversion while Rollo paid the *baksheesh* to slip into his jacket pocket the empty lemonade glass. The glass that Christabel Whipple had drunk from! He was determined to keep it as carefully as he looked after his cricket bat.

Because Corky Froggett was still with them – Rollo had said, 'The hell with protocol, let's get the poor blighter a drink' – Twinks did not communicate to Blotto what had happened down in the garage. But she was considerably surprised when Bengt Cøpper rejoined them, apparently unscathed by the experience of opening the sarcophagus.

'The contents are exactly what I would have expected,' he announced. 'Very satisfactory.'

But as he sipped his drink, remembering the Plagues of Egypt, Twinks watched him with anxious scrutiny, waiting to see his beer turn into blood.

It didn't.

# 23

# Breakfast on the Nile

The following morning they had breakfast served on the terrace of Twinks's suite at Shepheard's Hotel. She looked down at the distinctive blue of the river idling past them.

'Eau de Nil,' she said.

Blotto wrinkled his splendid nose. 'Is that what it is?'

'Sorry?'

'The odour.'

'No, not "odour". Eau de . . . Oh, never mind.'

When he was away from Tawcester Towers with his sister it never occurred to Blotto to have plans of his own. As a rule he just waited till Twinks told him what they were going to do. But that morning there was a level of transparent deviousness in his question, as he asked with elaborate casualness, 'Do we have any plans for the day?'

'I thought we were going to try to purchase a summer wardrobe for you.' Blotto had forgotten that, but as the heat of the day mounted he was already uncomfortable in his three-piece tweed suit. 'I don't think we'll have much luck in the souks for what you're after. Les Grands Magasins Cicurel, that's where we should go.' That was just the kind of information Twinks always had at her fingertips. 'Apparently they stock everything. Might even get your Old Etonian tie there.'

'Good ticket,' said Blotto.

But there was a nuance of reluctance in his tone which only his sister would have recognised. 'Why, do you have other plans?'

'Just fancied a stroll down to the Museum of Egyptian Antiquities,' he replied airily.

'Oh?'

'Always been keen on archaeology,' he continued.

'Have you, Blotters?'

'Oh yes. So I'd just like to stroll down to the Museum of Egyptian Antiquities and see what they have on offer there.'

'I'm sure you would, Blotto,' said his sister.


In the event a trip was made that morning neither to the Museum of Egyptian Antiquities nor to Les Grands Magasins Cicurel. Soon after a uniformed flunkey had come in to remove their breakfast trays (and been tipped for his pains), another uniformed flunkey appeared with a telephone message for Twinks. After he had been tipped, he handed it over to her. He waited while she read the message and then asked if there was any reply. She said no, but since he seemed to feel he should be tipped for asking the question, she tipped him again.

As soon as the flunkey had gone, Twinks offered the sheet of paper to Blotto. 'Bengt Cøpper's moved very quickly,' she observed with satisfaction.

It was a bit early in the morning for Blotto to concentrate on reading, so he said, 'Just give me the main headlines, Twinks me old backscratcher.'

'Bengt Cøpper has already identified the location of Pharaoh Sinus Nefertop's tomb. If Corky has the old Lag outside the hotel on the ping of eleven, he'll take us straight there.'

152

'And poor old Corky won't have to worry any more about Hail, Locusts, Darkness and the Death of the Firstborn.'

'Bong on the nose, Blotters. Hopefully the poor old pineapple's boils will clear up too.'

'Has he still got 'em, Twinks?'

'Had when I last asked.'

'He's a grade A foundation stone, isn't he – Corky? Never complains about anything.'

'Well, except about not having enough opportunities to lay down his life for us.'

'True.'

Blotto stretched his tweed-clad arms above his head in a gesture of relief. 'And then the whole clangdumble'll be sorted and we can pongle back to Tawcester Towers as quick as a lizard's lick.'

'Larksissimo!' But Twinks wasn't actually cheerful enough for a real full-bodied 'Larksissimo!' Though her brother seemed conveniently to have forgotten the fact, she couldn't be unaware of the situation that faced them on their return. The financial troubles of Tawcester Towers had not been resolved. The vultures were gathering and there was a very real threat that the estate might have to be sold and turned into an hotel.

What's more, their trip to Egypt, though it would undoubtedly have been of benefit to Corky Froggett, in other respects would have made things worse rather than better. The sarcophagus of Pharaoh Sinus Nefertop was the only thing of value that the Lyminster family possessed. The Dowager Duchess saw its sale as the route out of their pecuniary embarrassments. Twinks wasn't looking forward to the interview in the Blue Morning Room when she and Blotto told their mother that they had left the precious object in Egypt.

153

Still, it wasn't the moment for that kind of recrimination. Corky Froggett had to be released from his sentence of afflictions. Twinks turfed Blotto out of her suite, saying she needed to dress for their journey and agreeing to meet in the hotel foyer at ten to eleven.

Back in his own quarters Blotto also felt rather down, but the reasons for his gloom were different from his sister's. The fact was that – an almost unprecedented event – he had woken up in the middle of the night. With a feeling. A different feeling from the limited range which usually illuminated his psyche. Had he been more familiar with it, he would have recognised something called yearning.

He was yearning for Christabel Whipple. A woman as big as he was, who liked cricket and bore an uncanny resemblance to his hunter Mephistopheles ... what more could a boddo ask for?

He had decided back then in the middle of the night that he would go and visit Christabel the following morning at the Museum of Egyptian Antiquities. With that comforting thought in place, he had turned over in bed under his mosquito net and gone straight back to sleep.

So when the message had arrived in Twinks's suite from Bengt Cøpper, Blotto had been considerably cast down. His visit to the Museum of Egyptian Antiquities would have to wait. But he still did feel a very unBlottoish need to communicate with Christabel Whipple. And that led him to an even more unBlottoish decision: he would write a note to her.

Now Blotto had never been a whale on writing. Indeed, so reluctant was he to put pen to paper that some of his beaks at Eton had expressed the opinion that he couldn't actually write. The situation wasn't that bad but, generally

154

speaking, he would go to considerable lengths to avoid any kind of written communication.

That, however, was before he had become afflicted with this new yearning. He just knew that he had to make contact with Christabel Whipple that very day.

The desk in his suite's sitting room had a copious supply of Shepheard's Hotel embossed writing paper and Blotto got through quite a few sheets as he drafted and redrafted a message whose tone would suggest the depth of his feelings without making him sound too abject or needy.

The task took a while and it was twenty to eleven before he had created a formula of words that satisfied him.

He read them for the final time: 'Dear Christabel, Got to do business with Bengt Cøpper today. Hope your work at the Museum of Egyptian Antiquities is interesting. Hope we meet another day. Yours sincerely, Blotto.'

Though he said it himself, he was quite pleased with the result. It was the final sentence before the 'Yours sincerely' that had caused him most difficulty. Because that, he recognised, was the place where he was going to express the emotion that he felt for Christabel Whipple. He didn't want that emotion to come across as disrespectful or presumptuous so he knew he should be wary of laying it on with a butter knife, but he did want her to be aware of it.

He had rejected various other versions of that sentence. First he'd gone boldly for: 'You remind me of my hunter Mephistopheles', but he thought that might be too meaty for a well-brought-up English rose to cope with. 'I really want to see you again' also seemed a bit too raw. And 'I hope you feel the same for me as I do for you' was just asking for trouble.

No, he was very pleased with: 'Hope we meet another day.' If Christabel Whipple couldn't gauge the depth of his emotion from that, then she wasn't the sensitive creature that he had marked her down as.

He rang for a uniformed flunkey to organise delivery of the note. When the man had had his task explained to him, he said that of course he would need a *baksheesh* to do it. *Baksheesh* would also be required for the hotel's concierge, the other uniformed flunkey who actually took the message, the doorman who let that uniformed flunkey out of Shepheard's Hotel, the driver in whose cab he would travel, the doorman at the Museum of Egyptian Antiquities, the porter at the Museum of Egyptian Antiquities who would take the note to Christabel Whipple, the driver in whose cab the other uniformed flunkey would drive back to Shepheard's Hotel, the doorman who would let him back inside, the concierge to whom he would report his mission accomplished, and the further uniformed flunkey who would pass that news on to the writer of the note.

Blotto handed across the money.


He and Twinks met in the foyer as arranged. When they stepped out into the surprising heat of the day, Blotto wished there had been time to visit Les Grands Magasins Cicurel and stock up on a summer wardrobe. Bengt Cøpper looked a lot more comfortable than Blotto felt, in his dusty brown shirt, cotton trousers and leather hat.

Corky Froggett, standing beside the gleaming blue of the Lagonda, must have been feeling similar stickiness in his thick blue uniform, but of course he betrayed no signs of it. 'Have you still got the boils?' Twinks murmured to him as he opened the car door for her.

'Oh yes, milady,' replied the chauffeur as though they were a badge of honour.

It was agreed that Corky should drive, and Bengt Cøpper should sit beside him to give directions, with Blotto and Twinks in the back.

'Right,' said the archaeologist as the chauffeur pressed the self-starter and nosed his way gingerly through the floods of street children, 'let us return Pharaoh Sinus Nefertop to his rightful home.'

# 24

# The Return of the Sarcophagus

The road which took them out through the suburbs of Cairo was better than the one Blotto had driven down from Alexandria. It was almost clear of sand, so Corky Froggett did not have to go as fast as the young master had done on their previous journey. There was something almost sedate about the Lagonda's progress, fitting, Twinks thought, for the final journey of a pharaoh to his place of reburial.

Bengt Cøpper had a couple of maps open on his lap. The larger one, with many folds, was a commercially printed large-scale representation of Cairo and its environs. The smaller had been scratched out in pen on a scrap of paper. It was almost transparent along the folds and the Indian ink had faded to sepia.

'Are we going to the Valley of the Kings?' asked Twinks, a little breathlessly. The idea of actually being in that fabled location gave her quite a frisson.

'Of course, milady,' replied Bengt Cøpper, with the suave assurance of someone who had been there many times.

The greenness of the Nile-irrigated suburbs gave way surprisingly quickly to the sands of the desert, but still the road surface remained good and clear. Blotto didn't take much notice of the landscape through which they were driving. He just kept looking covertly at his watch, wondering whether Christabel Whipple would have received his note yet. And wondering how she would react when she did receive it. Had he been too forward with that 'Hope we meet another day' line?

He was pleased that he'd extracted his cricket bat from his valise back at Shepheard's Hotel and brought it with him. He stroked its battered, linseed-oiled surface, but it didn't bring the same quality of reassurance as it usually did.

They didn't seem to have been driving very long when Bengt Cøpper instructed Corky Froggett to take a minor road off the main one up into a craggy hillside. The surface of the road here was naked rock, but it seemed to have been much used and did not give them too bumpy a ride. A lot of red dust flew up around them, though.

When they crested the brow of the first hill, they saw spread before them an area that looked for all the world like a building site. Deep parallel trenches had been cut into the rock. Wooden scaffolding stood against unfinished walls. Primitive cranes, also made of wood, posed like giant wading birds. There were piles of gravel, sand, cement, with discarded tools lying beside them. Though the work appeared only recently to have been abandoned, they saw no sign of any labourers.

But, alerted by the sound of the Lagonda, two men in dark blue uniforms eased themselves up from the shade of a wall where they had been sitting and moved towards the approaching vehicle.

'Ahmet! Mustapha!' Bengt Cøpper called out as soon as they were in earshot. '*Salaam*! I am here as promised.'

He pointed out a flat area on the edge of the workings where Corky Froggett should park the Lagonda and they all decanted onto the bare rock. Without the motion of the car to cool them, they were aware of the sudden rush of

159

heat. Blotto felt sweat trickling down his tweed-clad back. He still held his cricket bat, swishing it aimlessly at imaginary bouncers.

The two men in uniform appeared to know the archaeologist, but their manner was hardly welcoming. Prominent on their belts were revolvers in heavy leather holsters. Prominent on their faces were the expressions of me who wouldn't think twice about using them.

'Before we can proceed,' said Bengt Cøpper, 'these two will require *baksheesh.*'

Twinks duly paid them from the dwindling stock of Egyptian pounds in her sequinned reticule. Then she looked around at the landscape in which they had arrived. 'Great whiffling water rats!' she said. 'So this is the Valley of the Kings?'

Bengt Cøpper smiled a harsh smile. 'You sound almost disappointed, milady.'

'Well, it wasn't quite what I'd imagined.'

'In what way?'

'I suppose I was expecting something more ... I don't know ... splendid.'

'All the splendour is buried underground,' said Bengt Cøpper. 'You were expecting rows of sarcophagi on display like in a museum, were you, milady?'

'No, I wasn't,' Twinks replied quite shortly. She was finding a little of the archaeologist's insolent confidence went a long way. 'It's just to me this looks more like the foundations of a spoffing great building rather than an excavation site.'

'And have you ever seen an excavation site, milady?'

Twinks was forced to admit that she hadn't.

'Then I think you should give me the benefit of the doubt on this one,' said Bengt Cøpper, only just on the right side of rudeness. 'I have spent my entire adult life in archaeology. And I can tell you this is a very typical excavation

160

site. What may look to you like new building is in fact work to shore up the walls of the ancient burial tombs. The fabric of some of them is much degenerated, affected by centuries of flash floods which have filled the chambers with debris. If you will be so good as to accept my expert view on the matter . . . ?'

Twinks bridled at his sarcasm, but she had no other arguments to put up against him, so instead she said, 'Well, for the love of strawberries, let's get on with replacing the sarcophagus, shall we?'

'Of course, milady. That is, after all, the reason for our presence here in the Valley of the Kings.'

'Yes.' Twinks looked around and observed something that seemed strange to her. 'I thought there were lots of tombs and excavations in the Valley of the Kings.'

'There are indeed, milady.'

She gazed across the reddish rocky outcrops towards the distant horizon. 'Well, I can't see any others.'

'Milady,' said the archaeologist with patronising patience, 'are you aware of the size of the Valley of the Kings?' Once again Twinks was forced to admit ignorance. 'Well, I can assure you it's massive.' He gestured to the highest ridge of rock. 'From the top of there you'd be able to see any number of excavations.'

Twinks didn't argue any more. She and Blotto watched disconsolately as Bengt Cøpper, closely consulting his worn handwritten map and a small compass, moved along the rows of cement-lined trenches. The sun stood directly overhead. Blotto's tweed suit was distinctly soggy. He had the sensation of being in a steam bath . . . and the equally uncomfortable sensation of being apart from Christabel Whipple.

Sweat, trickling from among the upright white hairs on Corky Froggett's head down his face, dripped from the promontories of his nose and chin. But he was too much of an old soldier to show any signs of discomfort (even with the boils).

'Here it is!' came a cry from Bengt Cøpper and he gestured the other three to join him. They moved across, shadowed by the two men in dark blue uniforms, and stood at the edge of a rectangular hole in the ground. Its floor and walls were of smoothly rendered cement. A cement-lined doorway led off to a smaller inner chamber. On the ground nearby lay a large rectangle of steel, clearly designed as a cover for the main chamber. Rings were welded into its sides to fit, presumably with padlocks, onto other rings around the rim of the chamber. When locked in place, the cover would frustrate any potential intruders.

'So this is the ancient burial chamber of Pharaoh Sinus Nefertop?' asked Twinks, her voice full of patrician scepticism. It looked to her more like a half-built wine cellar.

'Yes,' the archaeologist replied and waved the piece of paper in his hand. 'This map was copied directly from the papyrus of a notorious grave-robber of the first century BC. He knew where all the bodies were buried.'

'So why is this place encased in cement which looks not more than a week old?'

Bengt Cøpper sighed a long-suffering sigh. 'Milady, you have admitted to me that you have never been to an archaeological site, and here I regret you are just once again showing your ignorance. What were you expecting from the burial chamber? Walls richly painted with images of Egyptian gods and goddesses?'

'My researches into the subject have led me to expect something along those lines, yes.'

Another exasperated sigh. 'Of course such images are there. But when the debris of the tomb's caved-in roof had been removed, along with the rocks and alluvial silt that filled the chamber, those paintings were open to the burning Egyptian sunlight for the first time in over two thousand years. It is common archaeological practice to cover such treasures with a thin coating of a special mortar as a means of preservation. When the roof of the chamber is rebuilt, the mortar will be removed and then the underlying paintings can be subjected to serious academic analysis.'

Something about this still didn't ring true for Twinks, but Bengt Cøpper was the expert – and he'd come with the recommendation of Rollo Tewkes-Prudely – so she grudgingly supposed he must be right. And she did get a charge from being so close to the fulfilment of their mission. Once that fumacious sarcophagus was reinstalled in its rightful place, the Curse of Pharaoh Sinus Nefertop would be cancelled out. Corky Froggett would lose his boils and the threat of further afflictions, and the Tawcester Towers party could return home . . . to face the wrath of the Dowager Duchess. She tried not to think about the last bit.

'Now we're going to need some help,' Bengt Cøpper announced. He turned to the uniformed men and asked, 'I don't suppose you would like to give us a hand, would you?'

They agreed that they wouldn't. 'But we can find you workers . . . for of course a small *baksheesh*.'

More Egyptian pounds were produced from Twinks's sequinned reticule. Then one of the uniformed men put his fingers into his mouth and produced an ear-splitting whistle.

For a moment Twinks couldn't imagine where they had materialised from, but she quickly rationalised that the horde of white-clad workers who appeared at the summons must have been hiding from the midday sun in the shade of the trenches. They surrounded the group of Europeans, eagerly offering guided tours and the services of family members, as well, of course, as demanding *baksheesh*.

The uniformed men quietened them down by the simple expedient of waving their revolvers around. Then they selected six of the strongest-looking and sent the rest grumbling back to their trenches.

The final achievement of Blotto and Twinks's quest – the actual return of Pharaoh Sinus Nefertop's sarcophagus to its ancient resting ground – happened with a speed that was almost bathetic.

Corky Froggett drove the Lagonda as close as he could get to the chamber. The panels were slid back to reveal the car's hidden compartment. Exposed to the sun of its homeland, the human figure painted on the stone cover of Pharaoh Sinus Nefertop's remains seemed to glow with a new brightness.

Two of the primitive wooden cranes were brought up and proved surprisingly effective in lifting the sarcophagus out of its hiding place. Then, directed by Bengt Cøpper, Blotto, Corky and the six Arab workers acted as pallbearers and carried the ancient artefact to the edge of its chamber.

The sarcophagus, with four men each side taking the strain on the ropes, was lifted up and gently lowered into the chamber where it landed on wooden rollers. It was then guided into the inner chamber, where the rollers were removed from under it. The moment the sarcophagus found its resting place, the Arab workers burst into a rousing cheer, before demanding further *baksheesh* for a job well done.

After she had paid them off, Twinks turned to their chauffeur. 'Still got boils, have you?'

'Oh yes, milady,' Corky Froggett replied with pride.

# 25

# Christabel Whipple Smells a Rat

Bengt Cøpper decreed that the cover should not be put over the chamber until the day cooled down a bit. The sun-heated steel rectangle would have burnt even the hardened hands of the Egyptian labourers. He sent the six helpers back to their trenches.

'And now, milady,' he said with something like complacency, 'we must return to Cairo, where you will pay my fee and we will raise a glass to a job well done.'

'Good ticket,' said Twinks.

Corky Froggett closed the secret panels of the Lagonda and reversed it back to a place where it would be easier for the passengers to get in.

'Handles like a dream!' he cried gleefully to Blotto, 'now it's got rid of all that weight.'

'Maybe I should drive back to Cairo?'

'Whatever you wish, milord.'

And Blotto did wish it. The way he drove, in contrast to Corky Froggett's more sedate style, would speed up their arrival in Cairo. And his arrival at the Museum of Egyptian Antiquities.

It was while they were getting into the Lagonda that Corky noticed the approach of a small cloud of dust from the direction of the capital. As it got closer, the cloud resolved itself into a dusty, barefooted, white-clad Egyptian on a dusty motorcycle. He brought his bike to a gravel-scattering halt beside the Lagonda. 'Please,' he said, 'is there someone here named Blotto?'

'That's my name-tag,' said Blotto.

'Well, Mr Blotto *effendi* . . .' The man removed a brown envelope from the folds of his robe. 'I have a message for you.'

'Well, put a jumping cracker under it! Hand the thing over!' Blotto felt very anxious. The message had to be from Christabel Whipple. Would she be telling him to take a long jump from a short pier? Had his sentence 'Hope we meet another day' been too raunchy for her delicate English sensibilities?

The motorcyclist was holding the envelope in one hand, but it was the other, empty one that was thrust forward. He didn't have to ask for *baksheesh*; Blotto just thrust the money into his hand.

Safely in possession of the message, Blotto moved away from the curiosity of the others to read it: 'Whatever you do, stay where Bengt Cøpper has taken you. I will join you as soon as I can. Christabel.'

*Toad-in-the-hole*, though Blotto. Suddenly he was rolling in camomile lawns. He hadn't felt this excited since he had been about to go out to bat at number three in the Eton and Harrow match.

'You lot go back to Cairo!' he called out. 'I'm going to stay around here for a while.'

'Why do you wish to stay?' asked Bengt Cøpper suspiciously.

'Oh, just fancy a bit of air,' replied Blotto fatuously.

The archaeologist grunted. 'Well, I wouldn't advise you to be too curious. This is a very valuable site.' He barked out some words in Arabic to the uniformed men. 'If you stray too far, milord, from where you should be, these two gentlemen have orders to bring you back. And if their orders are not obeyed, they are not afraid to use their guns.'

'Tickey-tockey,' said Blotto.

He was aware of the puzzlement in Twinks's eyes as the Lagonda started its journey back to Cairo. He would have liked to explain the situation to her, but he didn't want to shout it out in front of Corky Froggett and Bengt Cøpper.

Besides, though he normally shared everything with his sister, there were some things so important that they had to remain secret. And he had a feeling that Christabel Whipple might be one of them.


Blotto was bored. And excitement made his boredom more oppressive. Though he was sitting up against one of the walls, with the sun so high it afforded little shade. His tweed suit was as wet as a facecloth in a bath.

He wasn't a man of many resources in this kind of situation. Some people of course would have read a book, but given that Blotto was into his sixth year of reading *The Hand of Fu Manchu*, that wouldn't work for him. Even if he'd had the book with him, which he hadn't.

Anyway, Blotto wasn't the kind of person who could lose himself in a book. He tried to think what in his life calmed him, what took his mind off things that were worrying him. It was hard to come up with an answer because in his blessed life he had so rarely been worried. But at that moment he was feeling distinctly twitchy, uncharacteristically nervous about seeing Christabel Whipple again.

Cricket! Of course – cricket! Whole days of his life had vanished when he'd been playing cricket. During a four-day match he thought of nothing else every waking hour. A game of cricket would stop him thinking about Christabel!

He looked across the reddish rock of the desert. There was a flat area a little way away from the excavations which could have been designed to be a cricket pitch. Be a bit hard certainly. Ball would bounce rather more than it might at Lord's, but Blotto could adjust his batting and bowling to accommodate the difference.

Yes, what a beezer wheeze! Thank goodness he'd kept his cricket bat with him. And as he reached randomly into his damp suit pocket, he was ecstatic to find a cricket ball. Couldn't think how it had got there. Maybe he'd found it walking through one of the copses near the Tawcester Towers cricket pitch and popped it in his pocket. Always a lot of lost balls from the sixes he skied in there.

So . . . got a bat, got a ball. There were enough scrap bits of wood around to improvise stumps and bails. All he needed was twenty-one other players.

Caught up in the enthusiasm of the moment, Blotto almost gambolled across to the trench into which the sarcophagus's pall-bearers had disappeared. He also was feeling the warm glow that came from doing a good deed. These poor Egyptian pineapples had actually had to grow up without any knowledge of cricket. How impoverished their lives must have been! How much richer their existence would be once they had been introduced to the game. (Blotto was also confident playing cricket would raise their moral standards. Boddos with the prospect of spending a day at silly mid-off had better things to do with their time than just lie around, constantly asking for *baksheesh*.)

The six labourers were lying in the shade in various degrees of wakefulness. A couple were smoking cigarettes, others chewing something, as Blotto began his call to arms. 'Listen, you chaps, I've just had a buzzbanger of an idea!

Now you lot probably didn't do cricket at the schools you went to, but don't you get crabwhacked about that. It's the kind of game you can pick up at any stage, and you'll then spend the rest of your life wondering why you didn't see the light earlier. And once you've mastered the laws of cricket, it's all creamy eclair. And once you start playing I guarantee you'll find it exactly your size of pyjamas. So come on, me old poached eggs, what say we give it a go?'

There was a silence. Six pairs of lethargic brown eyes fixed on him. '*Baksheesh,*' said one hopefully; then all the others joined in.

After he had paid them, Blotto returned rather disconsolately to his wall. He leant against it and moodily bounced the cricket ball on the horizontal surface of his bat. Was there any wonder the world was in the mess it was? So far as he could see, only when the people of every nation under the sun played cricket could there be any hope of improvement, any hope of a decent long-term future for the planet.

His uncharacteristic gloom was fortunately not allowed to last for long. Because he saw that a large cloud of red dust was moving towards the excavations from the Cairo direction. It wasn't moving as fast as the motorcycle had and when Blotto could discern its outline he could see why. The approaching mode of transport was a camel. And on its back, resplendent in dishevelled khaki, with a veil over her face against the dust, was Christabel Whipple.

He moved towards her across the desert rock. When they met, she slipped down off the camel, the halter still in her hand, and announced, 'Blotto, I can't tell you how pleased I am that you're still here.'

An expression of total bliss spread across his handsome features.

* * *

169

They were in the inner chamber with the remains of Pharaoh Sinus Nefertop. After her wonderful first sentence, Christabel's next had been an enquiry as to the whereabouts of the sarcophagus. And immediately she wanted to see it.

There was little light in the inner chamber, but Christabel Whipple, being almost as resourceful a young woman as Twinks, produced a large electric torch from her knapsack and ran it with interest over the surface of the sarcophagus.

Then she turned to Blotto and announced, 'Bengt Cøpper is a crook.'

'Is he, by Denzil?'

'Had I known he was the other archaeologist Rollo Tewkes-Prudely was introducing you to last night I would have warned you off straight away.'

'Does that mean the Major's a crook too?'

'I don't think so. I think Rollo's just a bit thick. In the next room when the brain cells were handed out. What's really wrong with him is that he imagines everyone else runs their lives by the same principles of British fair play as he does.'

'Oh well,' said Blotto, who fell rather into the same category, 'if that's a fault, it's a spoffing good fault, isn't it?'

'Maybe.'

'By the way, Christabel me old fruitbat,' he said, hoping he wasn't being too intimate, 'how did you know where to find me?'

'I telephoned Rollo this morning. Bengt Cøpper had told him where he was taking you. Though I would probably have guessed, anyway.'

'Oh?'

But Christabel Whipple didn't amplify her remark. Instead, she went on, 'You must be very careful, Blotto.

170

Bengt Cøpper is a dangerous major crook – and he's involved with a lot of other dangerous major crooks.'

'Don't don your worry-boots about me,' said Blotto with a hint of derring-do. 'I've got my cricket bat.'

'Hm. That might not be enough against the kind of weapons Cøpper and his acolytes favour.'

'Look, I'm sorry, I'm not on the same page as you, Christabel me old draining board. Could you uncage the ferrets about what's actually going on?'

'Yes. Presumably that bounder Cøpper told you this was the Valley of the Kings?'

'Yes.'

'Well, it isn't.'

Blotto was flabbergasted by this evidence of human perfidy. 'Broken biscuits!' he said. And he meant it. In some situations only strong language is adequate.

'Incidentally,' he went on, 'how did you know about the sarcophagus of Pharaoh Sinus Nefertop?'

'Rollo told me about it.'

'Ah.'

'By the way, you do realise that he's fallen in love with your sister, don't you, Blotto?'

'Yes.' He shrugged. 'Everyone does that.'

'Do they?' There was a note of wistfulness in Christabel Whipple's voice. If it wasn't so ridiculously unlikely, Blotto would have thought she was saying that it was not something she experienced so frequently. Though, with a woman who bore such a close resemblance to Mephistopheles, surely that couldn't be true. Men must be positively falling over themselves to fall in love with her.

Blotto was tempted to use this little springboard he had been offered for an expression of his own feelings towards Christabel, but he didn't think the moment was right. Instead he said, 'If this place isn't the Valley of the Kings . . . ?'

171

'Which it jolly well isn't,' Christabel asserted.

'. . . then this isn't the burial ground of Pharaoh Sinus Nefertop?'

'Certainly not.'

Blotto nodded thoughtfully. 'Well, that explains something.'

'What?'

'Why Corky Froggett's still got boils.'

Christabel was about to ask for elucidation of this unusual observation when they were both stopped in their tracks by a heavy scraping and rumbling noise.

They rushed through into the main chamber just in time to see the last rectangle of sunlight vanish as the metal cover was shifted into place. There was a series of clanks as the padlocks locked it in position.

Blotto and Christabel were trapped!

# 26

# Conflicting Reports

Twinks was no more settled on her return to Shepheard's Hotel than she had been when leaving what she still believed to be the Valley of the Kings. Too many odd things were happening. And she didn't trust Bengt Cøpper further than she could throw him. Also, what was the reason for Blotto suddenly deciding to stay out in the desert? And, above all, why had Corky Froggett still got boils?

Not that they seemed to be worrying the chauffeur at all. He was extremely pleased by how the Lagonda handled without its load of dead pharaoh on the way back to Cairo. Having deposited his two passengers, he had taken the car straight down to the Shepheard's Hotel garage where he busied himself adjusting the car's tyre pressure and making other refinements which would bring it back to optimal performance.

Bengt Cøpper left Twinks as soon as she had paid him his fee, which still seemed modest, another thing to re-animate her suspicions. He said he was off to the Museum of Egyptian Antiquities to check some documents before he returned to the excavation site. Twinks felt considerable animosity as she watched him stride cockily out of the hotel foyer.

She asked at reception whether there was any mail for her and, after the appropriate *baksheesh* had been given, she was handed two envelopes. The smaller one had no stamps, suggesting that it had been delivered by hand. She opened it straight away.

'Dear Twinks,' the message ran. 'I find myself in the awkward position of having fallen in love with you. You are quite simply the most ravishing creature on earth. Please can we meet again as soon as possible? With all the emotion my honest heart can hold, Rollo.'

She tore up both envelope and letter and dumped the remains in an elephant's-foot waste bin. The other envelope interested her much more. Its contents were a cablegram, which she decided she would read in the privacy of her suite.

It was, as she had hoped, from Professor Erasmus Holofernes, and its length suggested that when it came to cablegrams he didn't care about the expense. But its contents were something of a bombshell.

'Dear Twinks,' she read. 'Thank you for yours from Cairo, which caused me considerable confusion, not because of your question about the Riddle of the Sphinx (which can be easily answered), but because of its reference to a letter you received from me at Tawcester Towers.

'The plain fact of the matter is, my dear Twinks, that I didn't write any such letter. I know that when you and your brother came to visit me at St Raphael's I said I would do some investigation and get back to you as soon as possible, but the fact is I got rather waylaid by other matters. It is in the nature of research – or certainly research by someone with a brain like mine – that one's interests can easily be deflected to another subject. And what interested me in our meeting was not so much the sarcophagus of Pharaoh Sinus Nefertop as the nature of your brother. You may recall I mentioned doing some work on the hereditary

174

component in genius. And meeting you two siblings, the one so divinely gifted and the other so . . . so much less so, turned my previous thinking on the subject on its head. I have been revising everything I have written on the subject, with the result that everything else has been woefully neglected.

'Including, I regret to say, my investigations into Pharaoh Sinus Nefertop and his possible link to the Plagues of Egypt. *Mea culpa*, my dear Twinks, *mea culpa*.

'I will now of course drop everything else and concentrate – belatedly, I fear – on the problems which you mentioned.

'Incidentally, going back to the Riddle of the Sphinx (as I promised I would), the riddle most commonly known – "Which creature walks on four legs in the morning . . .", etc. has nothing at all to do with Egypt. It is part of the Greek legend of Oedipus, who outside the Greek city of Thebes provided the right answer and destroyed the Sphinx who guarded the entrance. Though the Sphinxes of Egypt – particularly the one at Giza – may be more famous, they do not have any riddles attached to them.

'Why incidentally, my dear Twinks, do you find yourself in Egypt? A very pleasant place for a sight-seeing holiday, I believe, but from what you said about the state of the Tawcester Towers finances I am surprised you can afford one at this juncture.

'Do pass on my good wishes to your brother, should he remember me (which, from what I gauged of his intellectual capacity, he may well not). And, as ever, I send you my deepest affection, Razzy.'

Twinks sat back on her sofa and looked out over the Nile. The cablegram had prompted so many reactions that it took a moment for her to organise them in her head.

But the predominant conclusion that emerged was that she and Blotto had been duped. They thought they had travelled to Egypt on the express instructions of Professor Erasmus Holofernes, but that now proved not to be the case. The letter that had arrived at Tawcester Towers and sent them off on their travels had been a fake. Holofernes had had nothing to do with it.

So who had sent the letter? Who was it who was so keen to get her and Blotto to transport the sarcophagus of Pharaoh Sinus Nefertop back to Egypt?

And why?


Blotto was torn between two conflicting emotions. He was imprisoned, which was fumaciously annoying. But if he had to be imprisoned, there was no one he would rather be imprisoned with than Christabel Whipple. Doing anything with her was pure creamy eclair. The situation was all very confusing.

It hadn't taken long for the heat of the sun on the metal cover to turn the outer chamber where they stood into an oven. The temperature in the inner room was slightly cooler, but still pretty unsupportable. Christabel, needless to say, had a water bottle in her knapsack, but its contents wouldn't last them very long. What might happen when the water ran out neither wished to contemplate.

'Better sip from the jolly old bottle,' said Christabel as she offered it to Blotto. 'Don't have the luxury of any glasses down here.'

'Well, actually,' he said, reaching into the voluminous pockets of his tweed jacket, 'I have got one.' And he produced the glass that he had taken from the Two Pharaohs Hotel.

'Oh, that looks familiar.' Christabel stared at him. 'Why did you pick that up?'

'Oh ... er ...' Blotto was deeply embarrassed. 'Never

know when a spare glass is going to fit the pigeonhole. I just ... er ...'

He could tell from the shrewdness in Christabel's eyes that she knew exactly why he had taken the glass, and that made him feel even more embarrassed.

He tried to get out of the gluepot by changing the subject. 'I heard a jolly good riddle once.'

'Did you?' asked Christabel with amused affection.

'Yes. Now let me get it right ... "What is the difference between a person who sells watches and a prison officer?"'

'I don't know.'

After a moment Blotto was forced to admit he didn't either. He wished Twinks was there to tell him how to ask the riddle properly.

But Christabel Whipple didn't seem to mind about the unresolved joke. Instead she relaxed and talked to Blotto about her childhood, about how her discovery of a Saxon hoard of gold on her parents' estate when she was five had triggered her lifelong love of archaeology.

Secure in the intimacy of their conversation, neither Blotto nor Christabel wasted any time in conjectures as to who had locked them in the underground chamber or what those people's intentions for them were. The two were very similar in temperament. They had both been brought up constantly to stiffen their upper lips, to 'rally round', not 'to make a fuss' and to 'do the decent thing'. In other words, neither of them had any imagination at all.

And for Christabel, though being locked in might be a bit of a bore, their incarceration did at least give her the opportunity to make a thorough examination of the sarcophagus of Pharaoh Sinus Nefertop. As she had announced to Blotto when they first met, archaeology was 'the absolute love of her life', so she wasn't about to pass up the professional opportunity fate had offered her.

177

So while she talked about her childhood, she examined the sarcophagus. Blotto just watched as she ran her torch beam along its surfaces, stopping now and then to write a neat observation in her notebook. As she became increasingly absorbed she grew silent. Blotto felt content in her presence, hot but very content.

Some of the time he couldn't help noticing that, to get a better view, she squatted on her haunches. Wonderful haunches she had. Again he was reminded of Mephistopheles.

Eventually Christabel Whipple stood up, closed her notebook and turned to face Blotto. 'It's a fake,' she announced.

'What!' He was thunderstruck. Amongst the surprises that he and Twinks had encountered since they found the sarcophagus, the one thing he had never doubted was its authenticity. That conviction might have wavered a bit when the other artefacts brought back by Rupert the Egyptologist had been denounced as counterfeit, but Mr McGloam – an expert from the British Museum, no less – had never doubted the provenance of the sarcophagus. Christabel's words were a major body blow.

'Are you sure?' he asked.

'Positive. I've seen enough of the real thing to recognise one that's leadpenny.'

'Toad-in-the-hole!' said Blotto. 'But my sister Twinks – who you met briefly last night . . .'

'Yes?'

'But she could read those things along the side . . . horrorgraphs . . . ?'

'Hieroglyphs?'

'That's the Johnnie! Anyway, she said they were genuine hiero . . . hiero . . . She said they were genuine.'

'Yes, they're genuine. But they weren't carved over two thousand years ago. I wouldn't be surprised if they'd been done in the last few months. Oh, skilfully done – and the whole things been skilfully aged and distressed ... but the fact remains it's a fake.'

'How do you know?'

'I could tell you, Blotto, but ... how much do you know about archaeology?'

'Nothing,' he admitted.

'Egyptian history?'

'Nothing.'

'The burial rites of the ancient Egyptians?'

'Nothing.'

'Then I think it would be better, Blotto, if I were to delay my explanation of why I know that this is a fake to some occasion when we're more relaxed.'

'Tickey-tockey.' He couldn't wait for a situation when he and Christabel were more relaxed.

'No, I think what we should do right now,' she went on, 'is open the thing and find out whether there are any human remains in it or—'

'No, we can't do that!' cried Blotto.

'Why ever not, old thing?'

'Because I really don't want you to end up suffering from Plagues of Blood and Frogs and Lice and Flies and Moron and Boils and—'

'Blotto ...'

'Yes?'

'What on earth are you blethering about?'

'Well, this may look like an ordinary sarcophagus to you—'

'An ordinary fake sarcophagus.'

'That's as maybe, but I still have to tell you that some really murdy things happen to anyone who opens it.'

'Oh yes, I read that,' said Christabel casually.

'What do you mean?'

'That's what it says in the hieroglyphs round that side.'

'Yes, that's where Twinks found them and she said that—'

'But it's complete balderdash. A lot of nonsense has been talked about pharaohs' curses – particularly since the discovery of Tutankhamun's tomb – but it's all rubbish invented by the gutter press.' She moved towards the sarcophagus. 'Now this is going to be heavy, Blotto, but I'm quite strong and I'm sure you are too, so—'

'So you really think it's safe to—'

'Of course it's safe, Blotto. Don't you trust me?'

'Of course I trust you, Christabel,' he said devoutly.

'Right.' She indicated the wooden rollers on the floor. 'If we both get hold of one of those and push upwards against the rim of the lid, I'm sure we can shift it.'

Blotto did as he was instructed. The two of them were very close as they heaved against the pole, trying to shift the massive lid. At first it seemed absolutely rock solid, sealed in position by its own weight, if nothing else.

'Come on, Blotto – one more try. On a count of three . . . One . . . Two . . . Three!'

This time it worked. The lid gave way, lifting perhaps a couple of inches. But as it did so, the steamy chamber was filled by the terrible shriek Blotto had heard before in the Tawcester Towers attic.

'I told you so!' he shouted. 'We've unleashed the curse again and it'll be Blood and Frogs and Lice and Flies and—'

'Oh, Blotto, do put a sock in it,' said Christabel coolly. 'Now come on, just lift the bally thing a couple more inches and we'll be able to slide it back.'

'But what about—?'

'Just do it, Blotto!'

He did as he was told. He rather liked Christabel Whipple being masterful.

This time they succeeded. They lifted the lid out of its groove and slid it back along the top of the sarcophagus.

The first thing Christabel focused her torch on was a small battery-powered siren with a string attached to the lid. As she pointed it out she asked, 'Still think the thing's genuine, Blotto? That little widget dates from the last ten years or I'm a Dutchman. Certainly wasn't installed two thousand years ago. But now . . .' Blotto could hear the excitement in her voice and feel the tension in her body '. . . let's see whose remains are inside.'

She moved the torch beam down the interior of the sarcophagus till it came to rest on its glittering pile of contents.

Ingots of solid gold. Each one stamped: 'PROPERTY OF US GOVERNMENT'.

It was the Tawcester Towers bullion.

# 27

# Captured!

Corky Froggett was extremely dutiful. Indeed his duty to
authority – be it His Majesty's Forces or the Lyminster
family – defined his entire life. So he had willingly done as
instructed in driving out to what he had been told was the
Valley of the Kings and back to Cairo. In the Shepheard's
Hotel garage he had willingly retuned the Lagonda to its
highest pitch of perfection.

But when he had discharged those duties, he allowed his
own priorities to assert themselves. And he set out on the
mission which from his point of view was the main purpose of his visit to Cairo – the search for dirty postcards.

Corky was not a natural tourist. His main interest in
other countries was how many of their nationals he'd
killed on military service and his total of Egyptians was a
disappointing none. Nor did he have any skills in – or
interest in learning – foreign languages. But there are
certain words and combinations of words which seem to
be understood in every tongue – a kind of global lingua
franca. 'Taxi' was one, 'telephone' another. And, as Corky
Froggett found that day in Cairo, 'dirty postcard' also did
the business.

He made his first enquiry to the receptionist at
Shepheard's Hotel. For this one he could use English. The

receptionist clearly recognised the words 'dirty postcard', but regretted that he could not supply any information on the subject until he had been given a *baksheesh*. That really annoyed Corky. He argued forcibly that tipping was something that one's betters did to their worses. Working people should show solidarity with each other. They should not demand extra payment from their equals simply for doing their jobs. Both the chauffeur and the receptionist made their living by the sweat of their brows. The purity of their working-class ethics could only be sullied by the exchange of tips between them. At times during his harangue Corky Froggett sounded like Alfred Sprockett at his rhetorical best.

Needless to say, none of these arguments had any effect on the Shepheard's Hotel receptionist. He was incapable of releasing any information about dirty postcards until he had been given a *baksheesh*.

Somewhat annoyed, the chauffeur strode out of the hotel foyer (refusing *baksheesh* to the obsequious doorman) into the battering heat of the Cairo afternoon. There he went up to the first white-robed Egyptian he saw and said the international words 'dirty postcard'.

The man replied immediately in broken English that he had a cousin who dealt in just such wares and if the gentleman would follow him, he would make the required introduction.

Corky Froggett, his good humour restored by the ease with which this step had been achieved, did as he was told and walked in silence behind his new friend. He did not notice two surly-looking men in dark uniforms detach themselves from the shadows of Shepheard's Hotel and follow some twenty yards behind them.

A more sensitive soul than Corky's might have responded with fascination and delight to the sights around him as he was escorted from the main broad boulevards of the city into a hinterland of narrow streets. His new friend led him through the maze, into the midst of throngs of robed men and veiled women. They passed endless stalls displaying multicoloured fabrics, jewellery, amulets, scarabs, shoes, bags, fresh fruit, vegetables and spices. These last filled the air with their sharp aromas, mingling with tobacco and roasted meat. The air was also busy with the cries of the street traders extolling their wares, the clang of metalworkers' hammers and the distant tapping of drums.

Almost anyone but Corky Froggett would have found the atmosphere exotic. He didn't notice it. His main concern was what kind of dirty postcards he would be offered.

His other concern was that their journey seemed to be taking an extraordinarily long time. He'd lost count of the number of turnings they had taken through the souk. There was certainly no way he could have retraced their steps. Eventually, like a child on a journey, he asked his guide, 'Are we nearly there yet?'

'Very nearly,' came the reply. 'My cousin's shop is just around the corner. Very good dirty postcards. Best in Cairo. Very cheap too. And very dirty. Dirtiest in Cairo. You will see, *effendi.*'

'Don't worry,' said Corky, mishearing him, 'I won't be offended. Takes more than a bit of filth to offend me, let me tell you. Some of the stuff that was passed around in the trenches . . . phwoar!'

'We are here,' announced the man, taking a sudden turn off the main alley.

Corky Froggett followed, gleeful with anticipation. But round the corner he did not see the expected shop, nor the expected cousin, nor the expected dirty postcards. He was in a shallow cul-de-sac, an angle made by two dusty red buildings, invisible from the passing hordes.

Realising it was a trap, Corky turned, just in time to see the two men in dark uniforms blocking his exit. Fighting machine that he was, he immediately took up a defensive stance, but at the same moment the man who had been his guide enveloped him with his arms. Corky resisted like a tiger, but before he could work a hand free, one of the uniformed men had produced a blackjack and brought it down heavily on the back of his neck.

The chauffeur's last thought before he passed out was regret that he hadn't seen any dirty postcards.

The three men carried their insensible burden through the alleys of the souk, constantly asking to be directed to a doctor, maintaining the illusion that Corky had just been taken ill (not that any of the passers-by seemed much bothered with what had happened to him). Then they suddenly turned off into an even narrower alley that led down to the riverside.

A *felucca* was moored, waiting for them. The three men trussed up the unconscious chauffeur, pinioning his arms behind his back and tying his ankles together with ropes. Then they tipped him over the gunwale onto the deck of the boat. With a wave to the crew, they stood on the bank and watched as the *felucca* sailed off towards the middle of the Nile.

Twinks was not the kind of person who let setbacks set her back. Her parents' total lack of interest in her as she was growing up had made her into a resourceful child. And that resourceful child had become an even more resourceful adult.

So though the discovery that her and her brother's journey to Egypt (carrying with them the risk of permanently alienating their mother) had been based on false

185

information might have daunted a lesser spirit, that was not the effect it had on Twinks. It made her extremely angry, yes, but more than that it made her determined to remedy the situation as soon as possible.

A quick analysis brought the realisation that she had two immediate options. Bengt Cøpper having been proved to be a crook, the first possibility was to confront the man who had introduced the stencher to her, Rollo Tewkes-Prudely. But Twinks's estimation of the Major was that he was stupid rather than devious, exactly the kind of man whom Bengt Cøpper would have found easy to dupe. Besides, she hadn't got the energy to cope with another amorous swain cooing all over her.

No, a much better option would be to consult Christabel Whipple. On their brief meeting the previous evening Twinks had been impressed by the young archaeologist (and had not been unaware of her effect on Blotto). Christabel might not only be able to shed some light on the murky background of Bengt Cøpper, her professional knowledge could also enable her to explain the mysteries surrounding the sarcophagus of Pharaoh Sinus Nefertop.

As ever with Twinks a decision was no sooner made than acted upon. She immediately rang for a uniformed flunkey and paid him a *baksheesh* to take a message for Corky Froggett. He returned some ten minutes later with the news that the chauffeur did not appear to be in the building, for which he was paid another *baksheesh*. Twinks then paid him a further *baksheesh* to arrange for a taxi to be ready in fifteen minutes at the main entrance of the hotel to take her to the Museum of Egyptian Antiquities. In the foyer she paid *baksheesh* to the receptionist who told her her cab was waiting, the doorman who opened the hotel door for her and the porter who opened the cab door for her.

The minute she got in, she realised that she was not alone in the back of the taxi. But before she had a chance to escape she felt a strong arm gripping her round the waist and a damp cloth being pressed against her face. Because she was the kind of person she was, before she passed out Twinks identified the smell on the cloth as formyl trichloride. Chloroform.

# 28

# Imprisoned!

Blotto didn't know how he'd got into the room where he found himself. His last recollection had been of quietly simmering in the underground chamber with Christabel Whipple and the sarcophagus of Pharaoh Sinus Nefertop. Then they'd been aware of sounds above them and something sweet-smelling being pumped into their space. Blotto had started to feel drowsy and . . . that was the last thing he remembered.

He seemed to be in a hotel room, he decided as he came to. It was still light, though whether the same day as when he had lost consciousness he did not know. The windows were closed, but not barred. But when he tried to move towards them he found he was handcuffed to the brass frame of a massive double bed. He tried to drag it towards the windows, but either it was fixed to the floor or just too heavy for him to shift. Blotto was well and truly snickered.

He lay back on the bed, feeling a little woozy. It was like the morning after a night getting seriously wobbulated, but he hadn't had any alcohol at the excavation site (or whatever it really was). He wondered what the gas was that had so effectively knocked him out.

His next thought was of Christabel Whipple. What on earth had happened to her? Despite the uncomfortable conditions in that underground chamber, being there alone with Christabel had been one of the most profound experiences of his life. He'd never felt so fizzulated.

But, he thought with mounting panic, she must have passed out at the same time as he had. Where was she? What had happened to her?

His ugly imaginings were interrupted by the sound of the door opening. He turned to see the entrance of two men in dark uniforms. Though they were not the ones who had been at the fake Valley of the Kings, they had a lot in common with them. The same pistols in holsters, the same surly expressions of men who wouldn't be afraid of – indeed would take great pleasure in – using them.

'Can you tell me what in the name of strawberries is going on?' demanded Blotto. 'I am a British citizen and I have been kidnapped! When the boddos in the British embassy hear about this, there'll be one hell of a stink! His Majesty's Government might even send a spoffing gunboat!'

The uniformed men were unmoved by his arguments (and not only because they didn't understand the language in which he was speaking). While one of them covered him with his revolver, the other opened one handcuff, released Blotto from the bed and snapped the cuff back on his wrist before he had time to do anything about it.

'Come,' grunted the other one in heavily accented English. 'They want to see you.'

Just before he was manhandled out of the room, Blotto managed to get a glimpse through the window. He could see the breadth of the Nile and, on the nearside bank a terrace of tables under umbrellas of a distinctively purple hue. His brain working more quickly than it frequently did, he deduced that he was being held in the Two Pharaohs Hotel.

* * *

189

Blotto's guards stayed behind as he was pushed into a room on the same floor. They closed the door and he found himself in what appeared to be the sitting room of a suite; doors led off presumably to the bedroom and bathroom.

But he hardly had time to take that in, so great was his shock at seeing, seated at a table, Mr Crouptickle and Mr Snidely. Between them lay Blotto's precious cricket bat.

And on the floor, piled high, were the ingots of bullion marked with the words: 'PROPERTY OF US GOVERNMENT'.

Both accountants were dressed in their customary black suits and their similarities to predatory insects seemed more marked than ever.

'Milord,' said Mr Crouptickle with insolent condescension, 'welcome to Cairo.'

'Huh,' said Blotto with the hauteur that had carried the Lyminsters through many predicaments since the time of the Crusades.

'And may I thank you so much for being our unwitting mule in smuggling this precious hoard . . .' he indicated the bullion '. . . into the country for us.'

'You absolute stencher!' cried Blotto. 'You told the Mater that you'd sold that lot and invested the proceeds in shares.'

'Which is what Her Grace had instructed me to do.'

'Yes, but clearly you didn't do it!'

'Which was a very wise move. The price of shares has fluctuated considerably in recent years, making them a very hazardous investment, whereas gold has maintained its value commendably well.'

This time Blotto didn't need to have the word 'investment' explained to him. 'The fact remains that you stole that bullion from the Lyminster family. It is ours by right!'

'Really?' asked Mr Crouptickle drily. 'Not according to what is engraved on the side of each ingot.'

Blotto was in no mood for discussions of relative morality. 'You lumps of toadspawn,' he said. 'Are you telling me that you set up this whole spoffing scheme to get the gold out to Egypt?'

Mr Crouptickle inclined his head as if accepting a compliment. 'That is exactly what we did.'

'But why?'

'Milord, the movement of currency from one country to another is not always an uncomplicated process. Various permissions need to be sought, various taxes and other levies paid. How much simpler, it seemed to me, to avoid all such complications. I knew, you see, that I could realise the value of the bullion easily once it had been brought out to Egypt – a task in the achievement of which you, your sister and chauffeur have proved so helpful.'

Blotto was silent for a moment as his mind slowly worked through the implications of this. Finally he asked, 'So you planted the sarcophagus in the Tawcester Towers attic?'

Another gracious nod.

'How in the name of Stanley did you manage to do that without any of us noticing?'

'You may recall, milord, that some months ago the Tawcester Towers plumbing underwent a degree of modernisation. During that time you and the rest of your family, unwilling to submit to the upheaval of having common builders in the house, adjourned to stay with the Duke of Melmont at Snitterings . . .'

'And it was then that you . . . ?'

'It was easy to arrange,' said Mr Crouptickle smugly. 'The British working man has always been susceptible to a little extra financial inducement.'

'You mean you bribed these plumber boddos to put the sarcophagus in place?'

'Exactly so, milord.'

'And you set up all those murdy things that happened to Corky Froggett?'

'Yes, and in that I must acknowledge the invaluable assistance of my colleague, Mr Snidely.' The two accountants exchanged smiles of self-congratulation. 'Having been infiltrated into Tawcester Towers on the spurious excuse of taking an inventory of the contents, Mr Snidely was uniquely placed to organise that sequence of unpleasant events.'

'All of which,' Mr Snidely added, 'were exceptionally easy to arrange, except for the lice, which did involve my getting hold of Mr Froggett's uniform while he was asleep.'

'So it was you who switched the water bucket for one full of blood, you set up the frogs and the lice and the flies and the moron . . . ?'

Mr Snidely acknowledged that these had all been his handiwork.

'But how on earth did you arrange Corky's spoffing boils?'

'It was our estimation,' Mr Crouptickle replied smoothly, 'that you would be on your way to Egypt before we reached the Plague of Boils.'

'But Corky has got boils!'

'Poor Mr Froggett,' said Crouptickle without much sympathy.

'But why did you want the bullion out here, anyway?'

'Egypt is a land of opportunity, milord. Thanks to the many archaeological wonders of the country, the tourist industry is ripe for development. But the kind of development required needs capital.' He gestured to the pile of bullion. 'Capital which you, milord, have very generously brought out for us.'

'So what kind of spoffing investment are you talking about?'

'Hotels, milord. This hotel where we are at this moment

192

has been built by a business consortium of which Mr Snidely and myself are a part. The building site which yesterday you so readily took to be the Valley of the Kings is the foundations of yet another hotel. Thanks to you, milord, Mr Snidely and myself are set fair to make a great deal of money.'

The mention of yesterday's events reminded Blotto of another preoccupation. 'Christabel Whipple!' he cried. 'What have you done with Christabel?'

'Miss Whipple,' said Crouptickle oleaginously, 'is completely safe. And she will remain safe, so long as she cooperates with us.'

'Christabel would rather cooperate with a posse of plague rats!' Blotto asserted stoutly.

'We will see about that. It's amazing how cooperative people can be . . . when the alternative is death.'

'You wouldn't dare kill Christabel!'

Mr Crouptickle smiled. 'Wouldn't we just?'

'Anyway,' said Mr Snidely to his colleague, 'don't you think we should proceed with the reason why we brought Lord Devereux here this morning?'

'A good idea, Mr Snidely.' Crouptickle turned a watery beam on Blotto. 'Now the hotel-building consortium in which we are involved does not only do business in Egypt. We are looking to expand into other countries until our reach stretches across the globe. And an area on which we are particularly concentrating at the moment is the British Isles. Which is where you come in, milord.'

'Sorry? Not on the same page. What for the love of strawberries are you talking about?'

'As you know, milord,' Crouptickle continued evenly, 'your family estate Tawcester Towers is on the verge of bankruptcy. The proposition has been put to your mother the Dowager Duchess – indeed, I put it to her myself – that she should sell up and allow the place to be developed as an hotel.'

'No Lyminster would ever agree to that!'

'No Lyminster would have much choice in the matter. The economic reality is far too real.'

'And are you saying it's your spoffing consortium that wants to develop the place?'

'How very perceptive you are, milord. We are of the optimistic view that over the years a good few properties whose aristocratic owners have run out of money will come on to the market. And we intend to snap those up too for development as luxury hotels. Mr Snidely and I stand to make a lot of money.'

'Never!' Blotto cried defiantly. 'The Mater will never sell Tawcester Towers!'

'We were thinking she might be persuaded to . . .' Mr Crouptickle slid a typewritten sheet of paper out of a folder on the table '. . . particularly if her younger son endorsed the proposal.'

'I'd never do that! I'm not the kind of stencher who'd sell his own family down the plughole! You could burn my hands off before I'd do that.'

'Really?' Mr Crouptickle smiled. 'An interesting suggestion. And one that might be arranged. Though I think we'll start with less violent means of persuasion.' He pushed the letter towards Blotto. 'So we all we need is your signature on this letter addressed to your mother.'

'I will never sign it!'

'No? Even if your unwillingness to sign might result in something rather unpleasant happening to Miss Whipple?'

'You wouldn't dare!'

'Oh, but we would, milord. I'm afraid Mr Snidely and I are not in the habit of being affected by sentimental considerations when we are trying to get our own way. After all, we are accountants.'

194

'But you won't hurt Christabel?'

'We certainly will, milord . . . if you do not sign this letter.'

'Give me a spoffing pen,' said Blotto miserably.

'I'm glad you've come to see sense, milord,' said Mr Crouptickle as he handed a fountain pen across the table. 'After all, what greater persuasion could the Dowager Duchess have to sell Tawcester Towers than knowing it was her younger son's dying wish?'

'"Dying wish"?' echoed Blotto.

# 29

# Released!

Blotto made rather a meal of trying to pick up the pen in his cuffed hands. 'Sorry, can't do it,' he apologised.

Mr Snidely rose from his chair and moved around the table with the key to the handcuffs and released one wrist. Blotto reached towards the fountain pen.

But that was only a feint. What he really grabbed was his cricket bat. Immediately reassured and emboldened by the feel of its familiar handle in his hands, he made an upward sweep which connected perfectly with the tip of Mr Snidely's chin. The accountant fell like a tree hit by a tank.

Mr Crouptickle rose from his chair, but he wasn't quick enough, as Blotto brought his bat down heavily on the back of the man's neck. He too slumped to the floor.

Blotto picked up the key to his handcuffs. He had also noticed a key on the inside of the door, on a ring from which hung two others. He snatched this as he burst out into the corridor.

The two uniformed men were smoking cigarettes. But not for long. The glowing stubs shot up into the air as Blotto's cricket bat connected with their chins. One suffered from a well-placed square drive, the other a reverse hook. They too crumpled to the floor and lay still.

Now to find Twinks and Corky Froggett. Not to mention Christabel Whipple!

As he had hoped, one of the keys on the ring turned out to be a master which opened every room he passed. All of the doors were on one side, so that the rooms had views over the Nile. The first three were empty, but he struck gold with the fourth.

Chained to a bed, just as he had been, lay his sister.

'Larksissimo!' cried Twinks, as he uncoupled her handcuffs. 'I knew you'd come and rescue me, Blotto me old trouser button!'

'Any idea where Christabel is?'

'No, but I'm sure Corky Froggett's in the next room. I've heard him snoring so much in the Lag while you were driving that I'd recognise that sound anywhere.'

She was right. In a matter of moments the chauffeur too was released. 'You're a welcome sight, milord,' he said. 'And if you're being pursued by villains, I would welcome the opportunity to fend off the attackers, with the likely risk of my laying down my life in the process.'

'That's very white of you, Corky, but I don't think I am being pursued at this precise moment. Come on, let's see if Christabel's in the next room!'

Their luck was in. Twinks now had the master key and she unlocked the door. The large blonde archaeologist was indeed there, also handcuffed to a brass bed. The moment of her release, she and Blotto fell instinctively into each other's arms.

When the four of them were back in the corridor, they took their bearings. There were stairs at either end.

'We need to get out of here as quick as cheetahs on skates,' said Twinks.

'Yes, but . . .' Blotto gestured towards the suite outside which lay two stunned men in uniform. 'All of the Tawcester Towers bullion is in that room.'

'What?' cried Twinks. 'How on earth did that get there?'

'No time to explain now. But we must get the goodies out.'

'Corky and I'll go and fetch the Lag,' said Twinks, practical as ever. 'Then we can load the stuff and make our getaway.'

'Be careful!' said Blotto. 'Crouptickle and Snidely own this hotel, so it's likely all the staff are in their pay.'

'Crouptickle and Snidely?' echoed Twinks. 'What in the name of snitchrags are they doing here?'

'No time to explain! You and Corky go and get the Lag! Christabel, you go with them!'

'I'm staying with you, Blotto,' said Christabel Whipple.

Given the pressures of the moment, he was only briefly aware that these were possibly the most wonderful words he had ever heard spoken.

Twinks and Corky Froggett rushed off down the stairs at the far end while Blotto led Christabel back towards the room he had broken out of. Tying up Crouptickle and Snidely, not to mention the two guards, seemed a good idea. Then they could wait till Twinks and Corky returned, load the bullion in the Lagonda and get the hell away from Egypt and back to Tawcester Towers. There was no doubt in Blotto's mind that Christabel Whipple would be coming with them.

The uniformed guards still appeared to be insensible on the floor of the corridor, so Blotto and Christabel went into the room. The two accountants had not got up, but they were moaning and beginning to stir. Blotto stripped off the silken ropes which tied back the curtains at the windows overlooking the Nile. He started to tie up Mr Crouptickle's wrists and ankles.

They were aware of sounds in the corridor, people moving about, muttered conversation. Placing a finger to his lips for Christabel's benefit, Blotto stopped his trussing and moved cautiously towards the door. At that moment a knuckle rapped on it sharply.

Blotto flung the door open, to find himself faced by some dozen men in the Two Pharaohs Hotel uniform. Some carried revolvers, others knives and cudgels.

'Hoopee-doopee!' cried Blotto, flexing the cricket bat in his hands. 'These are the kind of odds I like, Christabel!'

He surged out into the corridor. Flicks of the bat to left and right sent revolvers flying. Arabic cries followed the clatter of willow on bone. Christabel Whipple watched in an attitude of love-struck hero worship as Lord Devereux Lyminster, armed only with his cricket bat, sent his foes scattering into retreat. As the last few ran off down the stairs, he stood in the doorway, a glow of triumph on his impossibly handsome features.

So much was she concentrating on Blotto's derring-do that Christabel was not aware of the door behind her opening. Nor did she see Bengt Cøpper emerge from the suite's bathroom with a leather-covered cosh in his hand. Only when it was too late for her to do anything about it did Christabel watch helplessly as the blackjack was brought down hard on the back of Blotto's neck.

He fell like a toppled statue.

# 30

# The Final Voyage

While Corky Froggett had gone off to Shepheard's Hotel to fetch the Lagonda from its garage, Twinks had decided to keep watch in the Two Pharaohs, well aware now that it was owned by their enemies. Knowing that she might be conspicuous in her grey silk flapper dress, white silk stockings and cloche hat, she had reached into her sequinned reticule for a disguise she had packed there for just this kind of emergency.

She changed in the ground-floor ladies' powder room at the hotel and when she emerged in a full-length blue robe, black *hijab* and veil, no one looked at her twice. She decided that her best point of view would be in the foyer. There she could sit quietly and unobserved, waiting until Corky arrived with the Lagonda. She also had a good view of the main staircase, down which Blotto or Christabel Whipple might come once they had finished trussing up his victims. Twinks resigned herself to waiting.

But what ended her surveillance was something totally unexpected. She did indeed see Christabel Whipple coming down the stairs from the upper floors, but the young archaeologist was not in Blotto's company. She was closely attended by two men in dark uniforms who seemed to be virtually frogmarching her. Following closely behind, skeletal in their black suits, were Mr Crouptickle and Mr Snidely with Bengt Cøpper. Bringing up the rear were two more uniformed men, carrying something heavy wrapped in a carpet. Twinks assumed it must be some of the bullion that Blotto had said was in the suite upstairs.

Rather than coming to the main doors of the Two Pharaohs, this little procession went out the back towards the Nile-side terrace. They were not aware of the veiled woman in a blue robe who followed discreetly behind them.

There was a motor launch moored against the jetty at the end of the terrace. A gangway was let down from the side to let passengers embark. Along this Christabel Whipple was escorted on to the boat. Resistance to her uniformed captors was clearly useless, and Bengt Cøpper followed closely behind them.

Mr Crouptickle and Mr Snidely stood back while the carpet and its heavy contents were manhandled on board. Only when the four uniformed men were back on the jetty did the two accountants get on the boat. Within seconds the mooring ropes were cast off and the motor launch was on its way out on the bluish waters of the Nile.

And nobody noticed that, clinging to the back of the vessel just above the waterline, was a small blue-robed figure.

For the second time that day – or was it the next day? – Blotto returned to consciousness not knowing where he was. He wasn't on a bed; beneath his back was flat stone or cement. He was also aware of a splitting headache and a vague wobbliness. At first he thought this was a related symptom, but after a while he decided that the motion was genuine, a slight rocking accompanied by a regular chug of some kind of engine.

201

Blotto decided he was on a boat and presumably, given where he'd started the day – or was it the day before? – that boat was on the Nile.

But he couldn't see anything. At first he thought that was because he was still semi-conscious, but again after a while he came to the conclusion that he was in a dark place. And at least, thank goodness, he wasn't handcuffed or, so far as he could tell, restrained in any other way.

He could feel something lying on his chest. Not any-thing heavy. He moved his hands up to feel what it was and, to his great relief, recognised the contours of his beloved cricket bat. That really gave him a lift. Nothing could be totally bad for Blotto so long as he'd got his cricket bat.

He then stretched out his arms to assess what kind of room he was in. And very quickly realised that, whatever he was in, it wasn't a room. The space in which he was enclosed was much smaller than a room. He could only reach his hands about a foot away from his body before they encountered walls made of the same kind of stone or cement as the floor on which he lay. And reaching upwards, he soon encountered a very low ceiling of the same material. The ceiling seemed to be curved above him. As he felt along it, he found its shape was a larger version of his own body.

Finally Blotto realised the truth. He was inside the sar-cophagus he had once believed to house the remains of Pharaoh Sinus Nefertop.

Christabel Whipple was in a very unhappy situation. Seated next to Bengt Cøpper at a table in the saloon of the motor launch, she found herself opposite Mr Crouptickle and Mr Snidely and between them two men she had never seen before. One of them they all seemed to defer to as their boss. He repeated his question, 'Will you cooperate with us, Miss Whipple?'

'By "cooperate" you mean that I should go against all my instincts as an archaeologist?'

'Oh, I think that sounds a little self-righteous, Miss Whipple. We're just asking you to help us in the same way Mr Bengt Cøpper has been doing for some years.'

'Denying that there are any objects of archaeological interest on the sites where you plan to build your hotels?'

'Exactly that, Miss Whipple. You catch on very quickly.' The boss smiled at her. 'There will of course be a few other services we require of you . . .'

'Authenticating fake artefacts, so you can sell them at inflated prices to gullible tourists?'

'That kind of thing, yes.'

'And is that why you've got that fake sarcophagus on the boat? So that you can sell it off to some poor unsuspecting collector?'

'No, in that case, Miss Whipple, we feel the sarcophagus has served its turn. And rather than leave around something that could potentially be used as evidence, it is our plan very shortly to dump the sarcophagus over the back of the boat. It will become just another secret in the mud at the bottom of the Nile.' There was a silence. 'You still haven't said whether you will cooperate with us, Miss Whipple.'

'No, that's true. I'm thinking about your offer,' Christabel lied. She would no sooner work for this bunch of crooks than she would have her head shaved and join a nunnery.

'You would only be doing,' the boss went on, 'what Mr Cøpper has been doing for us very successfully for years. As has Mr McGloam from the British Museum.' He gestured to the man beside him. 'I don't know if you two have met, Miss Whipple . . . ?'

203

'I have heard of Mr McGloam by reputation in archae-ological circles.'

'Thank you, Miss Whipple,' said the gratified Scotsman.

'A reputation which I now know, since I find him here amongst a bunch of crooks, to be totally undeserved.'

McGloam looked considerably less gratified.

'To call us "crooks", Miss Whipple,' said Mr Crouptickle evenly, 'is ungracious of you. We are merely men of business.'

'Men of business who do not mind stooping to the shab-biest of criminal tricks.'

Crouptickle spread his hands wide in a gesture of help-lessness. 'All commercial enterprises have to conform to the ethics of the countries with which they do business. A little flexibility must be allowed in such questions of moral-ity. Anyway, Miss Whipple, I am sure that both Mr Cøpper and Mr McGloam can tell you, we are very generous people to work with. You will be very well paid for your services ... won't she, Bengt?'

The Norwegian agreed that she certainly would be.

'And you would be doing us a lot of good too,' the boss went on, 'helping in the creation of what will soon be a global hotel empire.'

'And betraying the values by which any self-respecting archaeologist should conduct their work.'

'Again you're sounding a teensy bit self-righteous, Miss Whipple. All you would be doing is playing your rightful part in the capitalist system.'

'A system I despise.'

'Oh, a lot of us despised capitalism when we were young. The lure of Socialism can be very attractive when you own nothing that you want to protect. Most people grow out of that kind of idealism when they discover how the world really works.'

204

'Do they? Well, I have not yet been infected with that kind of cynicism. And I hope I never will be.'

'Fine words, Miss Whipple. But are you seriously saying that you will not cooperate with us?'

'That is precisely what I am saying.'

'Well, that's rather unfortunate. Because you do know rather a lot about how our consortium works. Rather too much, one might say. And if you're not on our side . . . possessing all that knowledge . . . I'm not sure that we can allow you to survive, Miss Whipple.'

Keeping clear of the motor launch's propellers, Twinks had hauled herself up over the stern of the boat soon after they left the jetty. Ahead of her she could see the enclosed bridge from which the boat's skipper steered the vessel. He had his back to her and she wasn't too worried about the possibility of his turning round.

There was no one on the back deck, just the heavy bulk of Pharaoh Sinus Nefertop's sarcophagus – or, as she now knew, the faked-up version of Pharaoh Sinus Nefertop's sarcophagus. It had been tied round with two stout ropes and placed on the edge of a hatchway that led down into the interior of the vessel, where presumably she would find Mr Crouptickle, Mr Snidely, Bengt Cøpper and Christabel Whipple. Under the sarcophagus were wooden rollers, like those with which it had been manoeuvred in the place that wasn't the Valley of the Kings. Large stone blocks had been placed to prevent the huge artefact from shifting, either forwards into the hatch or back over the boat's stern.

Resourceful though she was, it was difficult for Twinks to form a plan until she had more information about the level of predicament she was in. She looked around the deck, noting with approval that there was a small dinghy hanging from davits above the churning propellers. That might be useful if she needed a quick getaway. There were also some stout metal boathooks stowed along the side of the deck. They too might have a purpose to fulfil in the plan that was beginning to take shape in her mind.

A bit more scouting out was required, though, before she could put any of it into action. She moved silently towards the hatch to go down and explore the launch's interior.


Blotto had tried shifting the lid of the sarcophagus. He had pushed up with his feet, he had crouched in the cramped space pressing with his back against the curved surface trying to force it upwards, but either the cover was too heavy or it had been sealed or tied down. He had tried hammering with his cricket bat at the junction where the lid met the bottom part, hoping to crack the seal, but without success.

One thing he did notice though, during his exertions, was that a little light was penetrating the sarcophagus. A row of small holes had been drilled into the cover, just above where his head would naturally lie. He was sure they hadn't been there when he had last seen the thing, in the underground chamber in what wasn't the Valley of the Kings.

He found this obscurely comforting. Whoever had imprisoned him in the sarcophagus had not wanted him to die of asphyxiation. Clearly they had other plans for him . . .


Twinks heard voices as soon as she stepped on the ladder down into the launch's interior. The proceedings were dominated by a voice she recognised, but would not in a million years have anticipated hearing in Egypt in the middle of the Nile.

He was saying, 'Well, if that's your decision, Miss

Whipple, I can only say I'm sorry for you. I've given you the chance of saving your life and you've thrown it straight back at me.'

'I cannot go against my conscience. I love archaeology too much to compromise my feelings for the discipline.'

'Admirable – if foolish – sentiments, Miss Whipple.'

'And now, if you'd excuse me, I'd like to go up on the deck and compose myself for . . . whatever lies ahead.'

'I have no objection to your doing that, Miss Whipple. But I should warn you that, if you think you will have a chance of escaping from this boat, I would put such notions out of your mind.'

'I have no such hopes. I know what my fate is to be. I just need to go and compose my mind, to make myself ready for it.' Christabel Whipple did sound rather magnificent, thought Twinks, rather like Joan of Arc.

Twinks knew Christabel was about to come out and meet her, so she just had a quick look inside the room to confirm the identity of the man who had been speaking.

She was right. No one could mistake that cottage loaf body – or the ginger moustache. The boss of this criminal conspiracy was none other than Alfred Sprockett, the man who wanted to represent Tawcestershire in the House of Commons. So much for his Socialist principles.

Christabel Whipple left the cabin and walked straight into Twinks. She was so surprised that there was a serious danger she might have let out a cry, but Twinks clapped a hand over her mouth and led her up on to the deck.

'Listen,' she demanded when they were in the open, 'where's Blotto?'

'I don't know. I haven't seen him since he was knocked out by Bengt Cøpper back in the Two Pharaohs. I assume he's back there, under guard.' A tear glinted in Christabel Whipple's eye. 'So I'll never see him again before I die.'

'Don't talk such utter toffee!' said Twinks. 'You're not

going to die! We're going to get out of this murdy situation! We'll soon be reunited with Blotto!'

And Twinks quickly outlined to Christabel her plan of escape.

'Gosh!' said the archaeologist. 'What a spiffing wheeze! When Blotto and I were locked in that chamber yesterday or whenever it was, he said you were the nun's nightie and, gosh, was he right!'

But Twinks had no time for compliments. Quickly she lowered the dinghy down from its davits so that it floated behind the boat ready for their escape. Then she said to Christabel, 'Now, look, I'll remove the stone that's keeping the sarcophagus in place and get out of the way as quick as a lizard's lick. You get those boathooks under the back and give it a hefty shove, which won't be difficult with it on the rollers. Then, if my calculations are right – larksissimo! – the weight of the sarcophagus falling down through the hatch will punch a neat hole in the bottom of the launch and send that load of stenchers to their watery graves. Meanwhile you and I will be in the tender, rowing like mad back to the Two Pharaohs to rescue Blotto!'

And Christabel Whipple actually said, 'Jolly hockey sticks!'

They did exactly as Twinks had planned. She moved the stone out of the way. Christabel, raising it slightly with the boathooks, pushed the heavy artefact forward and, as she did so, she cried gleefully, 'I'm longing to see you, Blotto!'

'I'm longing to see you too, Christabel!' came a voice from the falling sarcophagus.

The two women looked at each other in horror. With sickening certainty Twinks realised that the heavy load taken from the Two Pharaohs Hotel wrapped in a carpet had not been gold bullion.

'Oh no!' cried Christabel Whipple. 'Blotto's inside the thing!'

# 31

# At the Bottom of the Nile

But for the small detail of its sending her brother to a watery grave, Twinks's plan worked brilliantly. The sarcophagus duly launched itself down through the hatchway and its weight smashed through the bottom of the motor launch, sending a huge jet of water up through the vessel, which sank within seconds. None of its passengers had time to move out of the saloon and they all went down with the boat.

Twinks and Christabel meanwhile had leapt into the dinghy at the critical moment, cut loose from the launch and floated free in the turbulence caused by the sinking vessel.

The young archaeologist's face was a picture of desolation.

'Don't don your worry-boots!' cried Twinks. 'I've still got a few beezer wheezes left.'

And she reached for her sequinned reticule.

Blotto was quite shaken up and bruised by the sudden movement of his stone coffin. He didn't know what caused the crashing noises around him, but as the pace of his descent slowed he concluded that he must be free-falling in the waters of the Nile.

Then he felt muddy water dribbling on to his face and he realised that the drilling of holes in the lid of the sarcophagus might not have been such a generous gesture on the part of his captors.

He tried to console himself. He'd had a good innings. But even as he had the thought he knew he'd rather have had a slightly longer innings. It was like just getting your eye in and then being clean-bowled by a daisycutter. Still, the great Umpire in the Sky had clearly given His verdict and Blotto wasn't the kind of abject stencher who'd question the decision.

And at least he thought, hugging it to him, he had his cricket bat. He wished that he had Mephistopheles with him in the sarcophagus too. And the Lagonda. And of course Twinks. And, increasingly, Christabel Whipple . . .

Oh well . . . Heigh-ho . . .


Twinks took off her Arab robes and stripped down to underwear. Then, attaching the end of a fine ultra-strong silken thread to one of the tender's rowlocks, she fed the line out as, taking a very deep breath, she dived into the muddy blue waters of the Nile. Her sequinned reticule was hung around her wrist. It was from that she had produced the thread and the goggles she wore.

Twinks had calculated that the flow of the river would have taken the debris of the motor launch some way further downstream than the sarcophagus, so she knew where to focus her search.

She also knew she didn't have long to rescue Blotto. Or till her breath ran out. After one abortive underwater circuit she had to return to the surface to take in another gulp of air. Then she dived again.

This time she was lucky enough to distinguish a line of bubbles rising from below. Following them down, she felt rather than saw the outline of the sarcophagus, already beginning to sink into the soft mud of the Nile bottom.

Twinks felt around the outside of the shape and found that it had been tied with ropes. Reaching into her sequinned reticule, she produced a boning knife to cut these. But the problem of lifting the lid remained. Blotto might have been able to push the cover up, but there was no obvious means of communicating the need to him.

Feeling the pressure of her dwindling breath supply, Twinks reached into her sequinned reticule and produced a small hydraulic jack which she kept there for just this kind of occasion. She managed to introduce it between the main part of the sarcophagus and its lid and began to pump. At the same time she banged on the cover with a small hammer to try to alert her brother.

Blotto, who had just been slipping into insensibility as the water inside rose above his nostril level, responded, pushing up with both his arms and his legs. The lid shifted, then slid off the sarcophagus into the mud.

Blotto and Twinks clasped their arms around each other and kicked upwards, until the pair of them, lungs bursting, broke through the surface of the Nile.

## 32

# Escape!

When parting from Corky Froggett as he went off to fetch the Lagonda from Shepheard's Hotel, Twinks had given him the master key to the suites in the Two Pharaohs. Returning and not finding her there, the chauffeur had used his initiative and, stuffing them one at a time inside his blue uniform jacket, had transferred all of the ingots from Mr Crouptickle and Mr Snidely's room to the secret compartment of the Lagonda.

So when the exhausted Blotto, Twinks and Christabel Whipple finally rowed their dinghy into the jetty of the Two Pharaohs, everything was ready for their departure. And there to greet them was not only Corky Froggett, but also Rollo Tewkes-Prudely.

'Twinks!' he cried. 'I have missed you so much! I love you so much!'

'Oh, go and boil your head in balsamic vinegar,' she said wearily.

He went, his visions of flaxen-haired children melting around him.

They didn't want to hang about. Though all their enemies, led by the great capitalist hypocrite Alfred Sprockett, lay at the bottom of the Nile, the fact remained that the Two Pharaohs Hotel was the consortium's fiefdom.

212

When news of the accident got back there, the English group might well be in danger.

Twinks had put her silk dress, silk stockings and cloche hat back on over her wet underwear, but Blotto's tweed suit was soaked through. But he still agreed they should get out of Cairo as soon as possible. 'Right,' he said, grinning at Christabel, 'England, here we come! Hoopee-doopee!'

'But I can't come with you,' she said.

Blotto looked thunderstruck. Discreetly, Twinks gestured to Corky Froggett that they should melt away and leave the young couple to play this emotional scene on their own.

'Can't come with me?' Blotto echoed blankly. 'But hasn't the time we've spent together over the last few days meant anything to you?'

'Blotto, it's meant more than I can ever say.'

'Then what's the chock in the cogwheel? We can go back to England, we can be together forever. You'll love Tawcester Towers – best spoffing hunting in the world. We've got our own cricket ground too. And the Mater'll come round to you in time. She'd rather I was with someone, you know, with a bit more dynastic value, but we'll soften up the old fruitbat.'

Seeing the uncertainty still in Christabel's eyes, Blotto hastened to add, 'I'm not talking anything outside the rule book. I'm talking about twiddling the old reef knot in proper style. White wedding with three veg and all that rombooley.'

'Are you asking me to marry you, Blotto?'

'Of course I am, me old trout-tickler. You're the finest piece of womanflesh I've ever encountered. And what puts the cherry on the muffin is that you keep reminding me of Mephistopheles.'

'Who's Mephistopheles?'

'My horse. Finest hunter you'll see this side of Vladivostok.'

'Oh,' said Christabel, perhaps a little taken aback. 'But, Blotto, I can't marry you.'

''Course you can. Easy as raspberries. Lots of places you can buy white dresses in good old Blighty, you know.'

'I can't marry you, Blotto, unless you're prepared to live out here.'

'Out here?' His jaw dropped. 'In Cairo? *Abroad*?'

'Yes, Blotto.'

'But why?'

'Because my work is here.'

'What, your archaeology?'

'Yes.'

'Oh, don't worry about that. Lots of archaeology in England. They keep digging up stuff. Saxon burial mounds, ships, hoards of gold coins. You said that's how you got started, Christabel, finding a Saxon hoard of gold. It'll all be tickey-tockey. You can't move in England for archaeology.'

'But, Blotto, I'm an Egyptologist.'

'Yes, but it's all the same kind of guff, isn't it?'

'No, Blotto, it isn't.'

'Well, we could . . .' His noble brow furrowed as he tried to come up with a workable compromise. Then he beamed. 'We could live at Tawcester Towers, and come out here for a holiday every few years. And then you could check out your mummies and scarabs and sarcophaguses and—'

'I'm sorry, Blotto. That wouldn't solve the problem. I love archaeology. It's my life. Not just archaeology, but Egyptology. It's my work.'

Blotto was confused. Rather in the way that he couldn't understand why women should worry their pretty little heads about whether they had the vote or not, he couldn't imagine a woman actually taking her work seriously.

But he listened to what Christabel said next. 'Blotto, there is nothing I would like more in the world than to marry you . . .'

'Well, then—'

Christabel raised a hand to silence him. '. . . but the only way it would work would be if you were prepared to live out here with me.'

'*Abroad*?' Blotto repeated despairingly. Of course, if she put it like that . . . well, there was no contest.

'Oh, broken biscuits,' said Blotto.


He was very subdued as they travelled back to Alexandria. He let Corky Froggett do all the driving, which was a measure of how reduced he was in spirit. Twinks tried to say things to cheer him up, to describe the delights they would be returning to at Tawcester Towers, but even she couldn't lift him out of his slough of gloom.

In Alexandria, they took one of the ingots out of the Lagonda's secret compartment and sold it to an avaricious but mercifully incurious dealer. That ensured that their lunching and the hotels in which they stayed as they travelled through Europe were of a higher standard than they would have been relying on Twinks's *baksheesh*-diminished supply of sovereigns.

But even all those splendid meals didn't raise Blotto's spirits much.

At least the journey gave them opportunities to explain things. They had each only got partial elements of the saga of Alfred Sprockett and his consortium's perfidy, and by a lot of talking they managed to piece together the whole story. Twinks even decided that it was time to tell Corky Froggett the explanation for all the strange afflictions that he had suffered.

215

'Swipe me!' he said, when she'd finished. 'Plagues of Egypt? Whatever will it be next?'

'Well, if Mr Snidely had seen his sabotage all the way through,' Twinks replied, 'next you would have had Hail, Locusts, Darkness and the Death of the Firstborn.'

'Blimey O'Reilly!'

'Incidentally,' Twinks went on, 'there's one thing that I still can't really understand . . .'

'What's that, milady?'

'Well, most of the things they set up were fairly easily explained – substituting the blood for water, putting the frogs in the Lagonda, all that. What I can't understand is how Mr Crouptickle and Mr Snidely managed to give you boils.'

'They didn't give me boils.'

Twinks was affronted. 'But, Corky, every time I asked you about it, you said that you'd got boils.'

'Yes, milady,' the chauffeur replied. 'I always have boils.'

Corky was not as low as Blotto on the return journey, but he was a bit disgruntled. He had been all the way to Cairo and never had got any dirty postcards.

# 33

# Return to Tawcester Towers

It was late evening when the Lagonda arrived back at Tawcester Towers, so it was not until the following morning that Grimshaw apprised the Dowager Duchess of the prodigals' return. Neither Blotto nor Twinks were surprised to receive summonses to meet their mother in the Blue Morning Room.

Staring them down from her throne-like chair, the Dowager Duchess's features looked as unforgiving as ever.

'So,' she demanded, 'am I to be granted any explanation for your appallingly thoughtless and disloyal behaviour – travelling to Egypt when I had expressly forbidden you from taking such a course? What have you to say for yourselves?'

'Sorry?' suggested Blotto meekly.

'"Sorry"?' repeated the Dowager Duchess. 'I don't think that "sorry" is adequate to this disgusting breach of etiquette and betrayal of the family honour. Honoria ...' things were really bad when Twinks got called Honoria '... having been blessed with a modicum more intelligence and judgement than your brother, do you have anything to say for yourself?'

'All I have to say, Mater,' Twinks began stoutly, 'is that, putting aside for a moment the reasons why we went to

Egypt against your express instructions ... the fact is that we have returned from Egypt with all of the Tawcester Towers bullion which your man of business Mr Crouptickle claimed to have invested but had in fact stolen from you.'

'Oh,' said the Dowager Duchess. 'Well, that's all right then.'

And it was all right. Enough of the gold was sold to settle the estate's outstanding bills. The local shopkeepers, their ardour no longer fanned by the ferocious rhetoric of Alfred Sprockett, soon realised what a good relationship they had with Tawcester Towers and continued their customary practice of overcharging the Lyminsters for everything. (And when the election actually arrived, Tawcestershire reverted to type and returned a Tory.)

Nor did the worldwide chain of Sprockett's Hotels ever materialise. With all its principal strategists at the bottom of the Nile, there was no one left to develop the brand.

Gratefully restored to Tawcester Towers, Corky Froggett resumed his assignations with the kitchen maid. He also bought a camera and with her help started producing his own dirty postcards.

Twinks went back to her customary routine of turning down proposals from ever richer and more handsome amorous swains. A little bored, she started translating Dante's *Inferno* into hieroglyphs.

And Blotto, inevitably, spent a lot of time at the stables in intimate discourse with Mephistopheles. But now there was a new depth to their closeness. When he saw the hunter's head from certain angles he couldn't help thinking wistfully to himself of what might have been.